THE SUMMER OF '71

(BASED ON TRUE EVENTS.)

BY
HECTOR M. RODRIGUEZ

Copyright 2026
"The Summer of '71"
First Edition
Copyright © 2026 Hector M. Rodriguez
All rights reserved. No part of this publication may be reproduced, distributed, or transmitted in any form or by any means, including photocopying, recording, or other electronic or mechanical methods, without the prior written permission of the publisher, except in the case of brief quotations embodied in critical reviews and certain other noncommercial uses permitted by copyright law.

Library of Congress Cataloging-in-Publication Data
Rodriguez, Hector M
"The Summer of '71"/ Hector M. Rodriguez
p. cm.
ISBN: 979-8-9224655-5-6
1. Historical Fiction 2. Memoir 3. Military 4. Military Brats
Printed in United States of America
First Printing: — 2026
For permissions requests, email the author/publisher at:
hcsm@comcast.net
DISCLAIMER
This is a work of fiction. Names, characters, businesses, places, events, locales, and incidents are either the products of the author's imagination or used in a fictitious manner. Any resemblance to actual persons, living or dead, or actual events is purely coincidental. The information in this book is provided for educational and entertainment purposes only. The author and publisher assume no responsibility for errors or omissions. Neither is any liability assumed for damages resulting from the use of information contained herein.
10 9 8 7 6 5 4 3 2 1

ISBN- eBook — 979-8-9924655-6-3

Additional Books
by
Hector M. Rodriguez

What Happened to Joe French?

The Path Taken—A Father and Son
Journey on the Camino de Santiago

24 Stories—A Collection of Short Stories

The Awkward Optimist—A Guide to
Human Connection

A Story—The Essence of Humanity

Echoes of Wakening

"El Columpio"
(w/Rolando Rodriguez)

The Most Excellent Adventures of Bang
and Clang
(Austin Macauley Publisher)

24 More- A Collection of Short Stories

The Summer of '71
(Screenplay)

ACKNOWLEDGMENTS

THE SUMMER OF '71

Every book begins long before the first sentence is written. This one began on an army base in West Germany in a summer I have been carrying for more than fifty years. It belongs, first and always, to the people who were there.

FOR THE BRATS

You know who you are. You are the children who learned to say goodbye before you learned to drive. You moved every two or three years and started over in new schools, new neighborhoods, new countries, with the practiced efficiency of people who understood from an early age that roots are a luxury and that you can carry what matters in a backpack. You made deep friendships in short windows and then watched them disappear in rear-view mirrors and felt the particular grief of losing someone you had not finished knowing yet.

This story is for you. For the kids who grew up on bases in Germany, Japan, Korea, Italy, England, and everywhere else the American military planted its flags and its families. For the ones who spoke the local language before their parents did. For the ones who were neither fully American nor fully anything else, who belonged to a third culture that had no name and no country but was absolutely real. For the ones who measured their childhood not in towns but in postings, not in schools but in homecoming seasons on bases where everyone was always half-packed.

The four boys in this story are composites. They are built from memory and imagination and from the faces of every kid I knew who was doing the same quiet calculus: How much can I afford to care about this place before we leave it? The answer, I came to understand, is all of it. You can care about all of it. The leaving does not cancel the belonging. It only makes it more precise.

To every military brat who ever stood at a fence line and looked at the country beyond it with the particular hunger of someone who is never quite settled: this story was written for you, by one of your own.

FOR THE ACTIVE DUTY AND VETERANS OF OUR ARMED FORCES

The Summer of '71 is set on an American army base in the final years of the Cold War. The men and women who staffed those bases, and held that line through the long uncertain middle decades of the twentieth century, are the reason the story was possible at all. Their service is the ground the story stands on.

To the men and women currently

serving: you are doing something that most of your fellow citizens will never fully understand, not because they lack gratitude but because the experience of service — the particular combination of sacrifice, purpose, boredom, danger, camaraderie, and loss that defines military life — is genuinely difficult to convey across the civilian divide. This story tries. It does not pretend to capture combat. It captures what it felt like to be a child in the community built around the people who were prepared for it. That is its own kind of tribute.

To the veterans, especially those who served in Germany during the postwar decades: you kept a complicated peace in a complicated country on a complicated continent, and history has not always remembered that clearly. The Rhineland-Palatinate region where this story is set was not a glamorous posting. It was a long, often cold, often unglamorous vigil. You kept it. This story remembers you.

To the veterans of the Second World

War, now so few in number: you walked through a landscape that this story only touches the edges of. The bunker in these pages is fictional. The war that sealed it was not. The soldiers on both sides of that wall in 1945 were real men with real names and real people who loved them. This story asks its readers to hold that weight for a few hours. It is the least we can offer.

A particular acknowledgment is owed to the families of the fallen — to the sons and daughters and grandchildren of the men who did not come home from the Westwall, the Hürtgen Forest, the Siegfried Line. Your grief is woven into the landscape of the story. It is why the bunker matters. It is why the arrow on the wall matters. Some things stay buried not because we forgot but because we could not find a way to bring them back up without breaking.

FOR FAMILY AND FRIENDS

A book this long in the making accumulates debts that no acknowledgments page can fully settle. What follows is an attempt, offered with the full understanding that the people named here gave far more than these sentences can hold.

To my family, who have listened to versions of this story for longer than is strictly fair: your patience is a form of love, and I have not taken it for granted. You have heard the bunker described more times than any civilian should have to endure. You asked questions that made the story better. You let me disappear into the work when the work required it, and you were there when I came back out. A writer without that is a writer without a foundation. I have been lucky in my foundation.

To the friends who read early drafts and offered the particular gift of honest feedback: you know what the manuscript looked like before you saw it, and you know what it needed. Your marginal notes, your careful questions, your willingness to tell me when something was not working — these are acts of generosity that writers depend on and rarely thank adequately. Consider this my attempt.

To the teachers, coaches, scoutmasters, and mentors who shaped the boys and girls we were on those bases: you were doing something that did not always look important from the outside — running a troop, coaching a team, keeping a Scout room open on a Saturday afternoon — but which was, in fact, the whole thing. You were giving children a sense of permanence in a life structured around impermanence. Some of you are in this story, transformed beyond recognition. All of you are in the way we treat each other: with the kind of decency that is taught, not assumed.

FOR THE PEOPLE OF GERMANY

This story is set in your country. It asks your country to carry a weight that is not entirely its own — the weight of a war that ended twenty-six years before the events in these pages, but whose landscape and legacy were still very much present in the summer of 1971. The dragon's teeth in the fields. The concrete bunkers in the hillsides. The sealed walls. The one-armed men.

I want to say plainly: Germany in 1971 was a generous host to American military families. The Germans we knew — the farmers, the shopkeepers, the children in the village schools, the men and women who tolerated American teenagers on bicycles or snow sledding in their fields, American cars on their roads, American music from American windows at American hours — received us with a grace that we did not always deserve and did not always appreciate.

The character of Dieter Kreuz is my attempt to honor that grace. He is a man who made a promise to a foreign soldier he barely knew and kept it for years with no reward and no audience. He is fictional. But the quality he embodies — the German capacity for Pflicht, for duty fulfilled quietly and without display — is something I observed in the real people of the Rhineland-Palatinate, and it impressed me then as it impresses me now.

To the Germans who have worked, in the decades since the war, to reckon honestly with what happened — who have built memorials, opened archives, taught their children the full history, and sat with the discomfort of a national past that is genuinely hard to sit with — this story tries to meet that honesty with its own. The German soldiers in these pages are not villains. They are men who died in a war their country started and their generation did not choose. Werner Hess scratched "I loved her" in a concrete wall because he had nothing left but truth.

That is human. It belongs to no single nation.

The Pfälzerwald is one of the most beautiful places I have ever walked. The beech forests, the limestone outcroppings, the meadows where wildflowers run to the creek edges, the old stone villages along the valley roads — all of it is in the story, transformed into fiction but accurate in feeling. I have been a guest in that landscape. I have tried to write about it with the respect a guest owes a beautiful place.

Danke. For the country. For the patience. For Dieter Kreuz's question and the fact that there was an answer.

The Summer of '71 is a work of fiction. The base is real. The Siegfried Line is real. The dragon's teeth are real. The sealed bunkers are real. The weight of history in that landscape is as real as anything I have ever felt standing in a field in September with the birds gone quiet and the temperature dropping. My brat friends are real.

What the four boys found is an unanswered question. What it cost them and what it gave them and what they did with it and what it meant to be twelve years old in a foreign country in a summer that changed everything — that is as true as I know how to make it.

If you served, this is for you. If your parent served, this is for you. If you grew up on a base anywhere in the world and learned the particular discipline of loving impermanent things — this is for you. You are not footnotes. You are the whole story.

Hector M. Rodriguez
Corvallis, Oregon
2026

CONTENTS

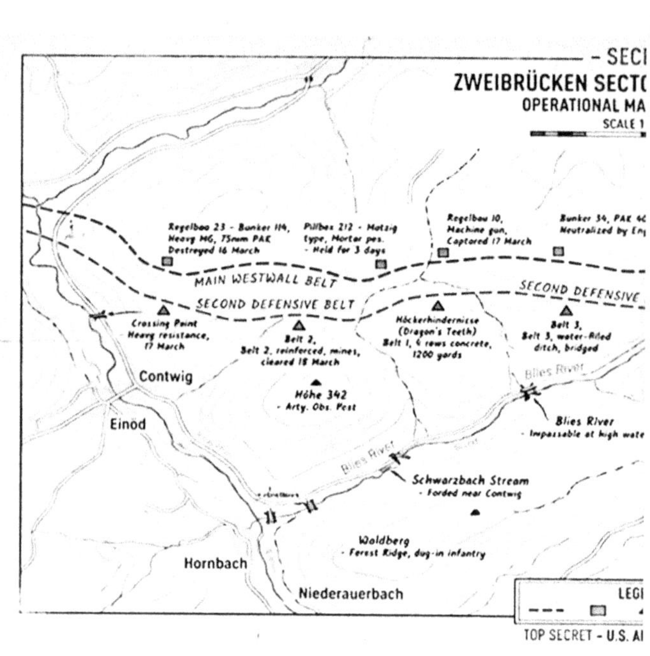
- SECI
ZWEIBRÜCKEN SECTO
OPERATIONAL MA
SCALE 1
Regelbau 23 - Bunker 114, Heavy MG, 75mm PAK - Destroyed 16 March
Pillbox 212 - Matzig type, Mortar pos. - Held for 3 days
Regelbau 10, Machine gun, Captured 17 March
Bunker 34, PAK 40 Neutralized by Eng
MAIN WESTWALL BELT
SECOND DEFENSIVE BELT
SECOND DEFENSIVE
Crossing Point - Heavy resistance, 17 March
Belt 2, Belt 2, reinforced, mines, cleared 18 March
Höckerhindernisse (Dragon's Teeth) Belt 1, 6 rows concrete, 1200 yards
Belt 3, Belt 3, water-filled ditch, bridged
Blies River
Höhe 342 - Arty. Obs. Post
Contwig
Blies River - Impassable at high wate
Einod
Blies River
Schwarzbach Stream - Forded near Contwig
Waldberg - Forest Ridge, dug-in infantry
Hornbach
Niederauerbach
LEGI
TOP SECRET - U.S. AI

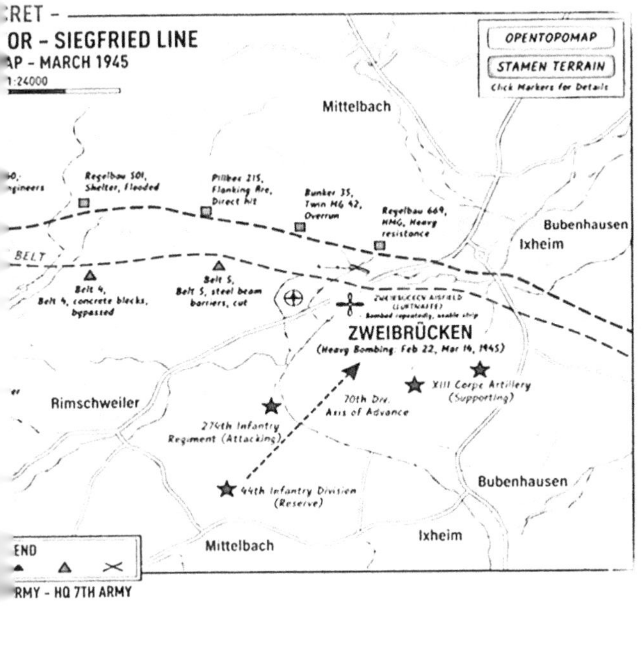
CRET –
OR – SIEGFRIED LINE
AP – MARCH 1945
1:24000
OPENTOPOMAP
STAMEN TERRAIN
Click Markers for Details
Mittelbach
Regelbau 501, Shelter, flooded
Pillbox 215, Flanking fire, Direct hit
Bunker 35, Twin MG 42, Overrun
Regelbau 669, HMG, Heavy resistance
Bubenhausen
Ixheim
0, Engineers
BELT
Belt 4, Belt 4, concrete blocks, bypassed
Belt 5, Belt 5, steel beam barriers, cut
ZWEIBRÜCKEN AIRFIELD (LUFTWAFFE) Bombed repeatedly, usable strip
ZWEIBRÜCKEN
(Heavy Bombing: Feb 22, Mar 14, 1945)
Rimschweiler
XIII Corps Artillery (Supporting)
70th Div. Axis of Advance
274th Infantry Regiment (Attacking)
44th Infantry Division (Reserve)
Bubenhausen
Mittelbach
Ixheim
END
RMY – HQ 7TH ARMY

Dedicated to
Bobby,
Rusty,
&
Pascal
and all the "Brats" around the world.

PROLOGUE

The Bunker at Kilometer 14
Siegfried Line — Southern Germany
March 16, 1945 — 0620hrs.

THE COLD CAME UP THROUGH THE
concrete like something alive.

Unteroffizier Klaus Bergmann stopped feeling his feet two hours ago. He
pressed his back against the eastern wall
of Bunker 1-14-Gamma and listened
to the world outside dying one artillery shell at a time. The floor trembled.
Dust sifted from the ceiling in thin
gray curtains. Somewhere to the south,
a fuel depot had been burning since
midnight, and the orange pulse of it

bled through the observation slit in slow, rhythmic waves, painting the interior of the bunker the color of a wound.

"Klaus." Private Werner Hess spoke from the observation post, his voice stripped of everything except the facts. "You need to see this."

Bergmann crossed the eight feet of concrete floor in three steps. He pressed his face to the slit.

The pre-dawn landscape unrolled before him — the cratered field, the torn wire, the skeletal remains of what had been the outer defensive belt. Three weeks ago this ground was fortified with men and purpose. Now it was archaeology. The pillboxes to the west had gone silent before dawn. The machine gun nest at the tree line stopped answering the field telephone at 0200. Between here and the horizon, the Wehrmacht existed only in memory.

And coming out of that memory, out of the brown morning haze, came the Shermans.

Bergmann counted them reflexively. Eight. No — ten. Moving in a loose wedge formation, their hulls dark with mud, antennas whipping. Behind them, shapes in the mist. Infantry. Dozens of them, spread wide, moving fast in short rushes from cover to cover with the practiced efficiency of men who had done this for a very long time and were very good at it and no longer thought about it consciously at all. They simply moved. They simply advanced.

"How many rounds do we have?" Bergmann said.

"Fourteen. For the Panzerfaust." Hess paused. "And I have my rifle."

"And I have mine."

Neither man said anything for a moment.

The lead tank — three hundred meters now, crossing the shallow depression where the anti-tank ditch had been — lurched as its left track found uncertain ground, then corrected and kept coming. The turret was traversing slowly, methodically, reading the fortifications the way a hunter reads a tree line. Looking for movement. Looking for the precise location.

"Werner."

"Yes."

"Did you write to Elsa?"

Hess lowered his binoculars. He was twenty-two years old and looked forty. His eyes were the color of old ice. "Three days ago. The last courier."

"Good." Bergmann picked up the Panzerfaust and checked it for the fourth time in an hour. "That's good."

Two hundred and fifty meters. The ground shook with the weight of them.

Bergmann had been on the Siegfried Line since November. He had watched the line contract around him like a fist slowly opening, each finger letting go. The Rhine bridgehead at Remagen had fallen six days ago — he'd heard it on the field radio before the field radio stopped working. The Americans were not stopping. They were not negotiating. They were simply coming, with their tanks and their artillery and their absolute industrial certainty that this was going to end exactly the way they had already decided it would end.

He understood this. He understood it since the Bulge collapsed in January. What he did not know was what to do with the understanding.

He stood in a concrete room with fourteen rounds and a rifle and Werner Hess, and he waited.

Two hundred meters.

"Now?" Hess said.

"Not yet."

The infantry had gone to ground, reading the bunker correctly, knowing that somewhere inside it a decision was being made. One of the Shermans angled toward them slightly, its 75mm gun dropping a degree, settling.

They see us.

"Klaus —"

"Not yet."

One-fifty. The tank's engine was

audible now through the concrete, a low grinding that Bergmann felt in his back teeth. The barrel of the 75mm was pointed directly at the observation slit. Directly at his face. He stared down it the way you stare at a thing you cannot look away from.

"Now," he said.

Hess fired.

The Panzerfaust round crossed the distance in a fraction of a second and struck the Sherman on the forward hull at an angle, and the shaped charge did exactly what it was designed to do, and the tank stopped. It simply stopped, like a clock winding down, and for one extended moment the world was absolutely silent.

Then it wasn't.

The remaining nine tanks opened up simultaneously. The bunker took the first 75mm round on the upper left corner, and the explosion was not a sound but a physical rearrangement of Bergmann's entire body, a concussion that threw him sideways into the wall and dropped him to his knees with blood running freely from his left ear. Dust filled the room. Something structural groaned above them. Hess was already at the second firing port, already working the bolt, firing at shapes in the smoke.

The second round hit the observation slit directly.

The slit was eight inches high and four inches wide, reinforced with six inches of steel on three sides, and the 75mm round found it with the indifferent precision of a war that had been going on long enough to become very good at killing men in concrete rooms. The blast came through the opening like a piston and stripped the observation post of everything standing in front of it.

Werner Hess had been standing in front of it.

Bergmann got to his feet. He did not look at what was behind him. He picked up his Karabiner 98 and moved to the secondary firing port on the south wall and worked the bolt and fired at a shape that was running toward him through the smoke, and the shape went down, and he worked the bolt again, and fired again, and the return fire was instantaneous and overwhelming and came from three directions at once, small arms and something heavier, and the secondary port was not reinforced the way the primary had been —

A grenade came through the ventilation slot.

Bergmann saw it land. A small, oblong American fragmentation grenade, wobbling slightly on the uneven concrete floor, its fuse burning with a hiss that was somehow the loudest sound in the world.

He was reaching for it when it went off.

The smoke was still drifting when Sergeant First Class Raymond Kowalski of the 3rd Infantry Division came through the bunker entrance with his Thompson at his shoulder and three men behind him.

"Clear!" someone shouted from the entrance.

"Check it," Kowalski said.

Private First-Class Thomas Albright went in first. His M1 up. He moved the way they'd all learned to move clearing confined spaces — fast, low, angles, corners — but there was nothing to clear. The room in the bunker was forty feet by twenty, tunnels trailing of in two directions, two dead Germans, and the wreckage of whatever the 75mm round had done to the observation post.

The smell was iron and cordite and something chemical from the tank that was still burning sixty meters away outside. Albright had been in enough bunkers by now that the smell didn't register as anything except bunker done.

"Two KIA," he called back. "No others."

Kowalski came in. The rest of the platoon flowed past the entrance, moving north, maintaining pace — they had an objective and a timeline and the Army did not pause for individual bunkers once they were neutralized. This was the math of advance: keep moving, keep pushing, don't let the enemy reset.

Kowalski gave himself sixty seconds. Not for sentiment. For intelligence.

He moved to the first body. German NCO, older, probably thirty-five, maybe more. Hard to say. The uniform told him rank; the dead told him nothing else. He checked quickly — no documents, but a map of the Westwall fortifications. He stuffed it inside his shirt moving to the second man. Young. Very young. Private, probably conscript. Nothing useful.

The bunker had already been stripped of anything valuable by whoever last re-supplied it. The radio — what was left of it — had taken shrapnel. The ammunition cans were empty. The field telephone wire had been cut from outside, deliberately, days ago.

Kowalski did a final sweep with his flashlight and that's when he saw it.

In the corner behind the shattered observation post, half-buried under a section of collapsed wooden shelf, was a canvas satchel. German military issue but personal, the kind of bag a soldier brought from home and carried alongside his kit. Someone tied it shut with a leather cord.

He crouched and opened it.

Four gold coins. Old, heavy — Reichsmarks. They caught the flashlight and threw it back with a warmth that seemed obscene against the concrete and the dead. He turned one over in his fingers and couldn't read the inscription but could feel the weight of it, the absolute specific gravity of something that had been valuable for a long time and would remain valuable for a long time after this particular morning was a footnote.

Beneath the coins, wrapped in a cloth that had probably been a handkerchief once, a Bible. German text, small enough to fit in a breast pocket, the cover worn to near smoothness. A photograph tucked inside the front cover — a woman standing in front of a house, squinting into summer sunlight, one hand raised to shade her eyes. No inscription.

And beneath that, in its flap holster, a Luger P08.

Kowalski held it up and worked the action. The mechanism was immaculate. Someone had maintained this weapon with a devotion that the war itself hadn't managed to erode. The grips were dark with handling. It was not a field weapon — or rather, it had been something else before it became a field weapon, something personal, something carried because it mattered.

He stayed crouched for a moment.

Outside, the sound of the advance was already moving north. Engines and boots and the distant percussion of a firefight opening up somewhere ahead. His platoon was sixty seconds from leaving him behind.

He thought about it the way he thought about a lot of things — fast and without sentiment, running the logic.

He couldn't take it with him. Not now. Not in this advance, not with the pace they were keeping, not with what was coming at Zweibrücken if the intelligence was right about the garrison size. He'd seen men get killed because they were carrying things they shouldn't have been carrying. An extra eight pounds of loot at the wrong moment.

But after.

He looked around the bunker. Found what he needed: Empty ammunition cans in disarray near the entrance, standard German 50 caliber, the kind that were built to seal. He grabbed one of the ammo cans and worked quickly. He wrapped the coins in the Bible's cloth covering, wrapped the Bible itself in a section of canvas torn from the satchel, wrapped the Luger in what was left. He packed everything tight into the ammo can, and locked the hasp. He found a section of the collapsed shelf with a natural depression in the earthen floor behind it, went down on one knee and dug with his hands until the hole was deep enough, and he put the can in, and he pushed the earth back over it, and he tamped it down, he replaced the section of shelf over it.

He stood.

He looked at the wall.

He took his Ka-Bar knife from his boot and crossed to the eastern wall — the cleanest section, the one least likely to take additional damage if someone shelled the ruins — and he etched it into the concrete with quick, practiced strokes, the lines cutting pale against the gray.

KILROY WAS HERE

He crudely marked an arrow pointing directly down to the floor. He stepped back and looked at it.

The letters were rough but legible.

Permanent. The kind of thing that would survive.

He picked up his Thompson.

He was through the entrance and moving north at a jog before the dust from the ceiling had finished settling.

The platoon had a 14-kilometer advance to consolidate before nightfall, and the village of Zweibrücken was waiting at the end of it with whatever the Wehrmacht managed to scrape together for a defense, and the morning was getting bright and cold and the Shermans were already half a kilometer ahead, pushing the road, and there was no time and there had never been any time.

Kowalski ran.

Behind him, in the bunker at Kilometer 14, the two Germans lay in the silence and the marks on the wall said what they always said, and the earth kept its secret with the absolute patience.

The war moved north.

CHAPTER 1

I have been trying to write this story since I was thirteen years old.

That summer — the summer of 1971, the summer in Zweibrücken, the summer Bobby Aldridge was still carrying his dead brother in his jacket pocket — I kept a journal. Pages of a green composition notebook, written in pencil because I was afraid of being caught and pencil erases. By September, I hid it in the bottom draw of my desk. I don't remember making the decision. I just remember the green composition paper and pages of secrets. I remember my father told us he was being reassigned again, and the prospect of leaving my friends, evoked a specific terror of a military brat who has lost friends to rotation before. In my mind, I quietly decided to stop making friends for fear of losing them, again.

I'm sixty-five now. I've written eight books. My first editor told me the best stories are the ones you're afraid to tell, and I have always believed her, and I have always been afraid to tell this one.

There were four of us. Bobby Aldridge, whose little brother Leo had been killed by a drunk driver in February — six months before that summer — and who had been wearing the same expression ever since: the expression of a boy who had been shown something about the world that couldn't be unshown. Rusty Abernathy, who was thirteen and red-haired and loud and secretly terrified that his last name meant something bad. Pascal Renard, who was half-French, half-American, who read German history books for fun, and who knew something about the Siegfried Line that he wasn't telling any of us. And me. The one who watches. The one who writes it down later and calls that the same thing as being brave.

It isn't, by the way. I know that now.

We were military brats — "brats" was the affectionate term, used by everyone including us, meaning children of U.S. service personnel stationed in foreign countries. Our fathers wore uniforms and our mothers wore the expression of people perpetually half-packed. We moved every two or three years. The friends you made burned bright and disappeared, and you learned not to say you'd miss anyone because missing people was weakness, and weakness was something you couldn't afford when your entire social architecture could be dismantled by reassignment orders. It was always "see you later" and then they were gone.

Zweibrücken, Germany. Summer, 1971. The army base, Kreuzberg Kassen, sat on a plateau in the Rhineland-Palatinate and smelled exactly like every other American military installation in the world. The air base sat across the valley on another plateau reeking of JP-4 jet fuel. Both carried crisply cut grass, a commissary's particular bouquet of canned goods and industrial floor wax. The F-4 Phantoms went over at 0600 every morning and rattled the windows, and by 0700 everyone was awake whether they wanted to be or not, and by 0900 we had exhausted all legal entertainment options, and by 0930 Rusty Abernathy would say, "I heard something," which was always how it started.

"I heard something," Rusty said.

We were sitting behind the bowling alley. It was the second week of July and about ninety degrees and Bobby was turning that smooth stone of Leo's over and over in his hands. Pascal was reading. I was doing nothing in particular, which I was very good at.

"About what," I said.

"About the bunkers out by the Siegfried Line." He leaned in. Rusty always leaned in. "My uncle says some of them were sealed before the Americans got there. With people still inside."

Bobby looked up. Slowly.

"People," I said. "Or bodies."

"Both, maybe." Rusty shrugged, performing nonchalance. "Does it matter?"

Pascal turned a page. He said, without looking up: "My grandfather fought near here. He said never open the sealed ones." A pause. He turned another page. "He said that twice."

We all looked at each other. The F-4s were making their noon run. Somewhere across the base a sergeant was yelling about something that had nothing to do with us.

"So," Rusty said. "You want to find one?"

What I remember about that moment — the moment I've been trying to write for forty years — is that none of us hesitated. Not really. Bobby said "yeah, okay" the way you agree to something you've been waiting to agree to. Pascal closed his book. I looked at the tree line beyond the perimeter fence, the dark fold of the Pfälzerwald, and felt something I could not have named at thirteen but understand now completely: the specific exhilaration of a door opening.

We didn't know about the gold yet.

We didn't know about the guard.

We just knew that we were bored, and that somewhere out there past the fence and across the hills and through the old dragon's-teeth fortifications of a war our parents never wanted to discuss, there was a door that nobody was supposed to open.

So naturally, we were going to open it.

CHAPTER 2

FIRST STEPS INTO THE WILD

WE LEFT ON A FRIDAY.

I know it was Friday because my mother made pancakes on Friday mornings — her one reliable weekly concession to something resembling a civilian life — and I lay in my bunk at four a.m. smelling the ghost of that morning's batch still hanging in the kitchen air, thinking: *in eight hours she's going to know I'm gone.* I thought about this with a clarity that surprised me. Not guilt, exactly. More like the sober arithmetic of consequence. She was going to be scared. That was a real thing I was choosing to cause, and I chose it anyway, and I have thought about that choice many times in the fifty years since.

I was twelve years old. I thought I was older.

My exit was the bathroom window — lower left corner pressure, slow lift, careful drop into the wet grass. I'd practiced it twice that week. The second time I'd done it in forty-one seconds, which seemed fast enough. I landed, went still, counted to thirty the way my father had taught me. Nothing moved. The base breathed and slept around me, the distant generators their own kind of silence once you'd lived with them long enough.

I found Bobby at the cracked oak, near Deadman's curve at four-seventeen.

He was already there. Of course he was. Bobby Aldridge had not been sleeping well since February, and everyone on the block knew it, and no one said anything about it because what do you say. He had his rucksack and his jacket and the stone in his jacket pocket, that smooth round river stone from Leo's room, and he looked at me the way he'd been looking at things all summer: steadily, carefully, from behind glass.

"Rusty," I said.

"Two minutes," Bobby said.

It was four minutes. Rusty arrived at a half-jog with his pack banging against his hip and his red hair doing something that suggested he'd slept on it wrong. He was breathing harder than the distance warranted.

"Sorry, sorry — the compass," he said, too loud. "I couldn't — I had it and then I—"

"*Quiet,*" Bobby and I said at the same time.

Rusty lowered his voice to a stage whisper, which for Rusty was approximately the same volume as a normal person talking. "The compass was under my mattress and then it wasn't and I had to check my dad's footlocker, which was locked, but I know where he keeps the key—"

"Rusty." Bobby's voice.

"Yeah?"

"Stop talking."

Rusty stopped talking.

Pascal came out of the hedge shadow without making any sound at all. This was characteristic. Pascal could apparently materialize from darkness whenever required, a talent he never explained and which we had stopped asking about. He looked at the four of us assembled in the pre-dawn grey and gave a single nod, the nod of a man who has been ready for some time and is patient about the fact that others weren't.

"Ready," he said.

We went under the fence at the weak spot — the bottom rail had come loose from a post and could be lifted about eighteen inches if you knew where to grip it. Rusty went first, then me. Bobby went third, deliberate and quiet. Pascal went last, and he lowered the wire back down behind him with the care of someone closing a door they planned to use again.

That sound — the small metallic click of the fence wire settling back into place — is one of the clearest sounds in my memory from that entire summer. I've heard it in dreams.

We were outside the fence. The rules stopped at the fence.

The German countryside in early morning is a specific kind of beautiful that I was not equipped, at twelve, to fully appreciate. Rolling hills going green and gold in the first light. Dark pine ridgelines. The damp, organic smell of fields that have been farmed for a thousand years. Mist in the low places, moving slowly.

What I registered at the time was: *Big. Open. No adults.*

We walked south-southeast per

Pascal's direction, no flashlights — there was enough grey light to navigate by, and lights could be seen — and within twenty minutes the base had disappeared behind a fold of ground and there was nothing in any direction that belonged to us or our parents or the United States Army. The world was old and indifferent and enormous, and the four of us were very small in it, and I would be lying if I said that didn't feel exactly like freedom.

Rusty felt it first, the way Rusty felt most things: loudly and entirely. He broke into a sprint across a meadow for no particular reason, his pack bouncing, and did a fairly poor cartwheel in the wet grass and came up grinning with his jeans soaked to the knee. "Let's *go!*" he said, and Bobby said "we *are* going," and Rusty said "no I mean *go,*" and there was something in this exchange that I loved, even then, though I wouldn't have been able to say why.

We walked through fields of

wildflowers that I couldn't name. We startled a pheasant out of a hedgerow — it exploded away from us at a speed that seemed genuinely alarming, a streak of colorful feathers, and Rusty shouted and Bobby laughed, the short surprised laugh of someone who didn't quite mean to. We crossed a stream on stepping stones and Rusty made a production of nearly falling in three separate times, only one of which I believe was accidental.

Pascal walked slightly ahead and slightly apart, which was his default formation. He checked his map at intervals, folded and refolded it along the same creases, and offered occasional quiet course corrections. "Bear left at the tree line." "There's a farm ahead — we go around, east side." He navigated the way good navigators do: without drama, without the constant reassurance-seeking that says *are we going the right way, are we still good,* just the steady accumulation of confirmed waypoints. The rest of us had already agreed, without quite saying so, that we would follow Pascal through anything.

For about two hours, it was perfect. That's the word. *Perfect.* Four boys in the morning countryside, no school, no parents, no schedule, the whole wide world available in every direction.

Then we found the dragon's teeth.

They came out of the earth at the edge of a long, low field, emerging from the grass in a row that stretched as far as we could see in both directions. Concrete pyramids, each one about waist height, stained with decades of rain. Pocked and scarred. Set at angles to trip up tank treads.

We stopped.

Rusty said, "What are those?"

"Anti-tank obstacles," Pascal said. "Dragon's teeth. Part of the Siegfried Line's forward defense belt."

"How many?" I said.

"This section? A few hundred, probably. Total — millions." He folded his map. "They built them along six hundred kilometers of border. The whole western frontier."

We walked among them slowly. The concrete was cold even in the morning warmth. Some of the pyramids had sunk at angles, listing into the earth like old headstones. One had been cracked open by frost expansion, and you could see the rebar skeleton inside, rusted orange, like exposed bone.

Bobby stopped and put his hand flat on the surface of one. He didn't say anything. He just stood there with his palm against the concrete.

"People died trying to get through these," he said.

"People died defending them too," Pascal said.

Bobby took his hand back. He looked at the line of pyramids going off toward the horizon, the way you look at something that goes farther than you expected.

"Let's keep moving," he said.

We'd been walking for five hours when Rusty jumped the gully.

The gully was maybe three feet across — a drainage cut in the field edge, steep-sided, maybe four feet deep. Nothing. The kind of obstacle a twelve-year-old clears without thinking.

Rusty jumped it the way Rusty did everything: with total commitment and zero preparation. He planted his left foot, pushed off, and his right foot caught the far lip at a bad angle. We all heard the sound.

It was a sharp, dense sound, like a green branch being forced the wrong way.

Rusty went down hard on his side and rolled twice and came to rest on his back looking at the sky with an expression of very controlled pain.

"Rusty—" I started.

"I'm fine," he said, from the ground.

Bobby was already beside him, kneeling. He moved Rusty's hand away from his ankle — Rusty had grabbed it reflexively — and looked at it without touching. "Can you move your foot?"

Rusty moved his foot and made a sound through his back teeth that was trying hard to not be a sound.

"It's not broken," Bobby said. "Probably. But you twisted it bad." He looked up at Pascal. "We need to rest."

Pascal had already found a branch — a good one, straight, about chest height — and was stripping the smaller branches off it with his knife. He worked without hurry. When it was done he handed the stick to Rusty without a word.

"I don't need a stick," Rusty said.

"Take the stick, Rusty," Bobby said.

"I'm not an old man—"

"*Take the stick.*"

Rusty took the stick.

He stood on the ankle with his jaw set

and went white for a moment and then the color came back. He took three experimental steps. "See," he said. "It's fine."

"It's not fine," I said.

"It's fine enough."

And the thing was — it was. Rusty Abernathy was many things, most of them loud, but he was not a quitter. He adjusted his weight onto the stick and he walked, and he kept walking, and he said "I'm fine" approximately every fifteen minutes for the rest of that day, and after a while we stopped responding because what was there to say. He was fine enough and we were moving and that was what mattered.

The farmer's dog found us around mid-morning.

We'd come to the edge of a cultivated field — someone's land, rows of something low and leafy that none of us could identify — and were picking our way along the fence line when the dog appeared at the far boundary: a big black-and-white sheepdog, already stiff-legged, already growling, its attention locked on us from sixty meters away like it had been waiting for exactly this.

"Don't run," Pascal said.

"I wasn't going to run," Rusty said.

"You were about to run."

"I was about to *walk quickly* in the other direction—"

"Same thing." Bobby's voice was quiet and steady. He was already gauging the distance to the trees. "Everyone still. Let it decide."

The dog had made its decision. The growl went up a register — a sound with commitment behind it — and it took two stiff-legged steps toward us.

Then the tractor engine, which had been a steady background rumble from the farmhouse end of the field, changed pitch. Dropped. Stopped.

"The farmer saw the dog move," Pascal said. "He's coming."

"Back," Bobby said. "Trees. Now. *Slow.*"

We backed into the tree line the way you back away from a dog that is deciding about you — no sudden moves, no eye contact, each step deliberate. The dog held position and kept up its warning. We hit the first cover and went still.

A figure was coming from the farmhouse direction. An older man, heavyset, wearing the kind of clothes you wear when your whole life is physical work. He stopped at the edge of his field and put his hand over his eyes and looked toward the trees.

We did not move. We did not breathe.

He looked for a long time. Long enough that I counted: one, two, three, up to twenty-eight. Then he gave a short whistle and the dog came back to him, and he stood a moment longer, and went back to his tractor, and the engine started again.

We stood in the trees until the tractor sound had been going steady for two minutes.

"He saw us," Rusty said.

"He saw four kids in the woods," Bobby said. "He's not calling the police about four kids in the woods."

"He might."

"He might," Bobby agreed. "Let's not give him another look." He turned to Pascal. "Alternate route?"

Pascal was already looking at the map. "A kilometer east. There's a wood line that should take us past the farm without crossing any open ground."

"How much time does that add?"

"Forty minutes. Maybe an hour with Rusty's ankle."

I looked at the sky. Still morning, plenty of day left. "Do it," I said.

We did it.

We found the shepherd's hut around two in the afternoon.

It wasn't much — stone walls, partial roof, the smell of old hay and a century of rain. The kind of structure that exists all over that part of Germany, too small to farm, too useful to demolish, just left in the landscape like a period at the end of a sentence. But it was out of the wind and the sky to the west had developed a grey thoughtfulness that none of us liked the look of, and Rusty's ankle had swollen enough that his shoe was getting tight, and we'd been moving for ten hours.

We stopped.

We ate half of what we had left — the crackers and the Snickers bars and the Vienna sausages from the C-rations, which tasted like metal and salt and something faintly chemical that we had all grown up eating and therefore associated with comfort. We drank from the stream that ran behind the hut. Rusty took his shoe off and looked at his ankle and then put the shoe back on without saying anything, which told me more than if he'd said something.

"How far?" Bobby said.

Pascal checked the map. "Three kilometers to the ridge. Maybe four. There's a descent on the far side, and then Kilometer Fourteen is at the base of the valley."

"Today?" I said.

Pascal looked at the sky in the west. "If we go now, we get there near dark."

"And navigate that terrain near dark with Rusty's ankle," Bobby said.

A beat.

"Tomorrow," Bobby said. "We camp here. First light, we make the final approach."

Nobody argued. The relief in Rusty's shoulders was visible to me, and I was the one who was always watching.

We made camp. "Camp" meaning we pulled the least-rotten pieces of the ruined roof structure away from the hut corner that still had a roof, and laid out our jackets, and designated a stream spot for water, and established that there was no food problem because we still had one more day's worth. Rusty spent twenty minutes constructing a small fire ring from the stones around the hut — his ankle propped, his hands busy with something — and we allowed this because Rusty needed to be doing something or he got loud.

The fire was good. Small, almost smokeless, the kind you can build when you've been a Scout, and the Scout leaders have drilled fire-building skills into you until it's reflex. The light it threw was warm and orange and it made the stone walls of the hut look like something from another century, which I suppose they were.

Bobby was turning Leo's stone in his hands. He'd been doing it all day and I'd been watching him do it all day. He'd found something earlier — a small lead toy soldier in the hut debris, one leg missing, the paint worn off — and he'd put it in his pocket alongside the stone without saying a word, and I'd filed that away too, the way I filed everything.

Rusty fell asleep before it was even fully dark. He didn't announce it. He was just there, and then he was snoring softly, his stick propped against the wall beside him.

Pascal was writing in a small notebook. His handwriting was cramped and precise and he tilted the book away when anyone got close, which was fine. Everyone had things they were keeping to themselves. After a while he stopped writing and looked at the wall.

"Pascal," I said.

"Mm."

"You said you'd tell us something. To-morrow. About what your grandfather said."

He was quiet for a moment.

"More than what you've already told us," I said.

"Yes." He looked at the fire. In the orange light he looked older than thir-teen. He looked like someone who'd been carrying something for a while and was working out whether to set it down. "There's a reason he said never open the sealed ones twice. Not just — not just the obvious reason."

"What's the obvious reason?"

"That there are dead people inside."

"Right."

"The other reason," Pascal said, "is that there might be things *with* the dead people. Things that were hidden there on purpose. Things people came looking for later."

"Came looking," I said. "Who?"

He didn't answer that directly. "My grandfather had a photograph. One photograph, of Kilometer Fourteen. He kept it in his bottom drawer and he took it out sometimes when he thought he was alone. I found it once, when I was eight. He didn't know." He paused. "There was an arrow scratched on the wall in the photograph. Pointing down."

I sat with this.

"He knew what was there," I said.

"I think he knew something was there," Pascal said. "I think he also knew that some things are best left where they are." He picked up a twig and threw it into the fire. It flared briefly and was gone. "I think tomorrow we're going to find out which kind of thing this is."

"And if it's the kind that should stay?"

Pascal looked at the fire. "Then we leave it there," he said. "And we go home."

He went back to his notebook. I lay back and looked at the partial sky through the ruined roof — a rectangle of black with stars in it, the Milky Way doing its thing, entirely indifferent to four boys in a German shepherd's hut thinking about things that had been buried for thirty-one years.

I thought about the arrow Pascal described — in his grandfather's photograph, pointing down at something. What? I wondered. Had been buried and left and not come back for?

That was all I knew. An arrow. A sealed door. A grandfather who said *twice* not to open it.

I fell asleep in the hut while the fire died and Rusty snored and somewhere in the dark Bobby turned his stone over

and over, and for some unknown reason, I dreamed about arrows that pointed
down.

I didn't know yet — wouldn't know
for another thirty years, until I found a
regimental history of the 3rd Infantry Division moving across the Siegfried Line
in a used bookstore in Portland and read
a footnote about the advance through
the western Palatinate — that the arrow
had been put there by an American sergeant named Raymond Kowalski, who
scratched it in thirty seconds and then
ran north to catch up with his platoon
while the war moved on.

But was the arrow there?

In the morning, we would find out if
it was.

I fell asleep thinking about that.

CHAPTER 3

THE APPROACH

WE WOKE TO BIRDSONGS, THE SOUND of the stream, a fresh pine forest sent, and Rusty saying he was hungry.

This was not a surprise. Rusty said he was hungry the way other people said hello — reflexively, as a form of greeting, as a way of establishing his continued presence in the world. But this time it landed differently because we were all hungry, and because the food situation had become, overnight, a genuine problem rather than a minor inconvenience.

I did the arithmetic while we packed

up the hut. We started with four days of supplies — C-rations, crackers, Snickers bars, the half-loaf of bread Bobby had taken from his family's kitchen at four in the morning with the specific guilt of someone stealing from people who love him. We had eaten well on Day One, the way you always eat too well on the first day when everything is an adventure and the consequences are tomorrow's problem. What remained was approximately a day's worth, rationed carefully. We had, by my estimate, at least two more days of walking ahead of us: today to the bunker, tomorrow home.

This math worked if nothing went wrong.

Bobby looked at the math the same way I did and didn't say anything about it, which was how Bobby communicated most things that mattered.

"We'll find something," Rusty said, with the easy confidence of a person who had not yet thought through what that meant.

"Such as," I said.

"Such as—" He waved a hand. "Berries. Wild stuff. Pascal knows plants."

Pascal, folding his map, said: "I know which plants will kill you. That's not the same thing."

"That's still useful," Bobby said.

We moved out at first light, south-southwest per Pascal's bearings. The morning was cool and clear, the sky that particular shade of blue that only happens before the heat of the day comes in and muddies it. Rusty's ankle had stiffened overnight and he was slower than yesterday, the stick doing more work, but he didn't complain and we didn't comment on it. This was the arrangement.

The countryside changed as we went.

It happened gradually at first — a concrete lump in the grass here, a suspicious mounding of earth there — and then all at once. We crested a low rise and the land below us was covered in them: pillboxes, dragon's teeth, tank ditches, the whole rusted-out infrastructure of a defense line that had been supposed to stop an entire civilization and had not. They stretched in every direction, half-swallowed by thirty years of grass and vine and German weather, but unmistakably there. The scale of it was staggering. Someone had built all of this. Tens of thousands of people had poured concrete and strung wire and aimed guns through narrow slits, and then the war had moved on and left it all standing, going slowly back to earth.

"The Line," Pascal said.

We didn't say anything. There wasn't much to say.

Bobby walked up to the nearest pillbox and put his hand flat against the concrete, the same way he'd touched the dragon's tooth yesterday. He stood there a moment.

"Do you do that with all of them?"

Rusty said. Not unkind. Genuinely curious.

"It helps me remember they're real," Bobby said.

Rusty considered this. "Yeah," he said. "Okay."

We went on.

What we didn't know — what I didn't learn until much later, years later, when my mother finally told me the story in the kitchen of her retirement apartment in San Antonio, her hands wrapped around a coffee cup — is what was happening behind us while we walked.

By five o'clock on Day One, the four sets of parents had done the math and found it came out wrong. My mother called Bobby's mother. Bobby's mother had already called Rusty's. Someone had tried Pascal's house and gotten no answer. By six o'clock the Military Police had been notified, and by seven there were two search teams moving through the sectors east of the base, which was the wrong direction entirely, but how were they to know.

My mother said she spent that first night sitting in the kitchen with the light on, listening to the house. She'd made my bed three times. I don't know why. She couldn't explain it either when I asked.

We were asleep in a shepherd's hut eight kilometers away, and we didn't know any of it. I have thought about that gap many times. The gap between what they were feeling and what we were feeling. We were scared too, in our way — the good kind of scared, the kind with momentum in it. But they were scared the other way, the still kind, the waiting kind, and there is no good version of that.

I'm sorry, Mom. I really am. Though I know saying it now, forty years later, is a little late to be useful.

Around midmorning we came to a village.

"Village" is generous. It was eight or nine buildings clustered around a crossroads, with a church whose steeple had lost its top at some point — wartime, probably, though it could have been weather — and a baker's shop with a wooden sign that had a pretzel painted on it and the smell coming from inside was something close to criminal, given our circumstances.

We stood across the road in the tree shadow and looked at it.

"No," I said.

"I didn't say anything," Rusty said.

"You were about to."

"I was about to suggest we buy something. Totally legitimate."

"With what money?" Bobby said.

A pause.

"Okay," Rusty said, "so not *buy* exactly—"

"No," I said again.

"Galen." He turned to face me with the expression of a man about to make an airtight legal argument. "We are going to pass out from hunger before we get to the bunker. We will literally collapse in a German field and never be found. Is that what you want?"

"Nobody is going to collapse—"

"My blood sugar is extremely low, I can feel it—"

"You had crackers an hour ago—"

"Those were Pascal's crackers and he gave me half of one—"

"*Half* of one was what you took, there's a diff—"

"*Boys,*" Pascal said.

We stopped.

Pascal had been watching the baker's shop with the systematic attention he gave everything. "The woman goes to the back room every fifteen minutes or so to check the ovens," he said. "She was just back there. We have about twelve minutes." He paused. "There are two loaves cooling on the front shelf. The smaller one."

Rusty pointed at me. "*He's* the fast one."

"I hate all of you," I said.

This was not true, but it felt true while I was crossing the road in what I hoped was a casual manner, my heart going at approximately twice its normal rate, my eyes on the doorway of the baker's shop and the dark interior beyond it and the two loaves of bread on the wooden shelf just inside.

The loaves were dark pumpernickel, dense and still warm. I took the smaller one — not because I was feeling particularly principled, but because the smaller one was closer and I was not going to be in that doorway one second longer than necessary. My hand closed around it. I turned. I walked back across the road.

I did not run.

I wanted to run so badly.

I crossed back into the tree shadow

and the three of them were looking at me with a range of expressions — Rusty with naked delight, Bobby with something harder to read, Pascal with the neutral appraisal of a man tallying a result.

"Go," Bobby said quietly.

We went.

We didn't stop until we'd put a full kilometer between us and the village, and then we sat in a beech wood and divided the bread into four equal portions and ate it with the specific intensity of people for whom food has stopped being ordinary. Warm pumpernickel with the crust still crackling. I have eaten in good restaurants since then, ordered from menus in four languages, had meals that cost more than my first car. I don't remember any of them as well as I remember that bread.

"Okay," Rusty said, with a mouthful. "That was worth it."

"We're not doing it again," I said.

"Probably."

"*Definitely.*"

"Sure," Rusty said, and ate his bread.

Bobby was looking at his portion. He ate slowly, the way he did everything that summer — with attention, like he was making sure to notice it. After a while he said: "Leo liked pumpernickel."

Nobody said anything.

"He'd put butter on it and then ate around the edges first. He said the edges were the best part." He paused. "He was wrong about that. The middle's the best part. But I never argued with him about it."

He ate the rest of his bread starting from the middle.

We found Elodie by accident, the way you find most things that matter.

It was early afternoon, and we had

drifted somewhat west of our intended line — following a creek bed that was easier going for Rusty's ankle than the slope above it — when the terrain opened into a wide meadow where the creek met a larger stream coming down from the ridge. The border was somewhere nearby; Pascal had mentioned it that morning, the way the Siegfried Line crossed and re-crossed the frontier in this area like someone had drawn it in a hurry.

She was kneeling by the water's edge with a woven basket beside her, her back to us, picking wildflowers with the unhurried attention of someone who has done this many times. Her hair was the color of summer straw. She was humming something. It wasn't a song I recognized.

We stopped.

Rusty opened his mouth. Bobby put a hand on Rusty's arm, which shut him up more effectively than anything else could have. We stood there at the edge of the meadow for a moment, the four of us, watching her.

She turned around.

She was maybe our age — twelve, possibly eleven. Her eyes were the particular light blue of faded denim, and she looked at us with complete calm, the way you look at something that has appeared in your meadow and that you are deciding about. She took us in — our dirty clothes, our too-heavy packs, Rusty's walking stick, the general condition of four boys who had been sleeping outdoors — and she said, "Bonjour."

"Bonjour," I said, which exhausted most of my French.

"Bonjour," Rusty said, and then, apparently deciding he had nothing to lose: "Parlez-vous anglais?"

She thought about this. "Un peu," she said. A little.

Pascal stepped forward. His French, it turned out, was considerably better than his modesty had suggested. He spoke to her for a moment, something low and rapid, and she answered, and her face changed — not alarmed, not unfriendly, just more interested. She gestured at the meadow, at the ridge above it, said something that included the word "village."

"Her name is Elodie, Elodie Moreau." Pascal told us. "She lives in the village below the south ridge. She comes here most days for flowers." He paused. "She says we look hungry."

"We are hungry," Rusty said immediately.

Pascal said something to Elodie. She laughed — a quick, unguarded sound — and reached into her basket and produced a cloth bundle, which she unwrapped to reveal a wedge of yellow cheese and a heel of bread. She held it out to us with both hands, the offering gesture of someone who does not need to be asked twice about generosity.

We ate the cheese and bread standing in the meadow while she went back to picking flowers and Pascal sat on a rock nearby and they talked, quietly, in French that the rest of us couldn't follow. Rusty sat with his ankle elevated and looked at the sky. Bobby waded into the stream up to his ankles and stood there with his eyes closed.

At one point Elodie picked a red poppy from the meadow edge and crossed to where Rusty was sitting and held it out to him with a small, serious expression. He took it, caught off guard. He looked at the flower and then at her and said "Merci" with such careful pronunciation that Elodie laughed again, and Rusty — Rusty Abernathy, who walked through life like he owned it — went slightly red.

He tucked the poppy behind his ear and wore it there for the rest of the afternoon.

Bobby, coming back from the stream, saw it and didn't say a word. But the corner of his mouth moved.

We stayed perhaps forty minutes. When Elodie stood and gathered her basket and said her goodbyes, she turned to each of us in turn and said something — something short, the same short phrase to each of us. Pascal later told us it meant: "Be careful in the hills."

We watched her go until the meadow folded around her and she was gone.

"Well," Bobby said.

"Yeah," I said.

Rusty touched the poppy behind his ear carefully, the way you touch something you don't want to damage. He didn't say anything, which for Rusty was its own kind of statement.

We shouldered our packs and went on.

The afternoon was harder than the morning.

The terrain rose steadily as we moved south and west, the easy farm fields giving way to rocky pasture and then to real forest — old growth, the kind of dark, dense pinewoods that make you feel the sky is a rumor. The ground was rooted and uneven. Rusty managed it, but the ankle was costing him, I could see it in the set of his jaw. He didn't say he was fine, which was how I knew it was getting bad.

The Siegfried Line was everywhere now. We couldn't go fifty meters without encountering a concrete remnant — bunker foundations, observation posts, machine gun nests with their narrow slits still aimed at approaches that tanks had stopped using a quarter century ago. The sheer density of it was different from the scattered dragon's teeth of the morning. This had been the main line. This was where the fighting had concentrated.

The light came through the pines at a low angle, and in that light the old concrete looked almost organic, like something that had grown rather than been built. I found myself watching the shadows between structures for movement and then telling myself to stop watching for movement and then watching again anyway.

"It's quieter," Bobby said.

He was right. The birds that had been constant company all day had dropped out. Wind in the pines, and our footsteps, and nothing else.

"We're getting close," Pascal said.

We made camp on the ridge as the sun went sideways through the trees.

Pascal's map said Kilometer Fourteen was less than a kilometer ahead, down the far slope, in the valley where the western approach road had run in 1944. We could see the ridge's far edge from where we sat, the land dropping away into shadow. Beyond it: the bunker. The sealed door. The arrow in the photograph.

Tomorrow.

Rusty built another fire while Bobby went to find water and I checked the remaining food, which was not a cheerful exercise. We had crackers enough for breakfast and nothing else. Whatever tomorrow brought, we were going home hungry or not at all.

When Rusty came back from gathering wood, he sat down and dug in his pack for a moment and came out with something small that he turned over in his hands. I recognized it: his father's belt buckle, brass, worn to a soft dull shine.

He didn't say anything. He started cleaning it with a corner of his shirt, the small circular motion of someone who has done this before.

"Your dad's," I said.

"Yeah."

Bobby came back with the water and set the canteens down and sat across the fire. He looked at the buckle and didn't ask.

"He did something," Rusty said, "in Korea. With a communications relay when half his unit was down. Kept it operational long enough for the advance to go through." He kept rubbing. "They gave him a commendation. Nobody here knows that. They just know about the other stuff."

I thought about the whispers that followed the Abernathy name around the base. The way certain parents said it. The way Rusty's shoulders changed shape when he heard it said that way.

"So come home with something better," I said.

He looked up.

"That's what we're doing," I said. "Right? You find something real, something nobody can take a side-eye at. It's yours."

He looked at the buckle. Then he put it back in his pack.

"It's not about the gold," he said. "I mean — yeah, obviously the gold would be incredible. But it's not—" He stopped. Started again. "I just want one thing that happened to me, that's mine, that nobody else's story is attached to." He poked the fire with a stick. "You know?"

"Yeah," I said.

"Don't say yeah like you feel sorry for me."

"I don't feel sorry for you."

"Good." He sat back. "My ankle really hurts, by the way. I've been not saying that all day."

"We know," Bobby said.

"Right. Okay." He stretched the ankle out carefully. "Figured."

Pascal, who had been sitting slightly apart looking at the valley below, spoke without turning around. "Tomorrow," he said. "We go down at first light. The approach is through the tree line — there's a natural drainage that runs past the structure. We follow it." He paused. "When we get close, I need everyone quiet. The terrain around the bunker — my grandfather described it. He said it had been worked on after the war. Cleared. And he said—" Another pause. "He said it had been visited. Not by historians. By others."

The fire popped.

"What other?" Rusty said.

"He didn't say." Pascal finally turned from the ridge. His face in the firelight was careful, controlled. "He said never open the sealed ones. And he said it twice. I've been thinking about why he said it twice."

"And?" I said.

"And I think the first time was a warning about what's inside." He looked at each of us. "I think the second time was a warning about who else might be looking."

None of us said anything to that. The fire went down and Bobby put another branch on it and we watched the sparks climb and disappear into the dark. Bobby tried wrapping Rusty's ankle that first night with a torn strip of his undershirt, but the material was too thin and too short, and by morning it had slipped

Somewhere below us, in the valley, the bunker waited.

Rusty's poppy was wilting in his jacket pocket, the stem bent. He took it out and laid it carefully on a flat stone beside the fire, like an offering, or maybe just like someone who didn't want to lose it.

I wrote none of this down that night. I had stopped keeping the journal two days in. But I remember it. I remember all of it. The fire, the four of us, the ridge, the darkness below.

The last ordinary night before everything that came next.

CHAPTER 4

KILOMETER FOURTEEN

We ate the last of the crackers at first light.

There's a specific flavor to crackers that have been in a canvas pack for two days in summer heat — a warm, slightly stale flatness that coats the inside of your mouth — and I ate mine slowly, making them last, listening to the forest come alive around us the way it did every morning. Birds first, then insects, then the small stirring of wind through the canopy. The sky above the ridge went from black to purple to a grey that promised blue eventually.

Bobby ate his crackers and drank from his canteen and checked the stone in his pocket. Present and accounted for.

Rusty ate his crackers and didn't say he was hungry afterward, which told me something. He was looking at his ankle with the expression of a man assessing structural damage he already knows is bad and is deciding how much to admit. The swelling had taken up most of the extra room in his shoe. He hadn't unlaced it because he was afraid if he took it off he wouldn't get it back on. He learned that in scouts.

"Don't say it," he said, without looking up.

"I wasn't going to say anything," I said.

"You were constructing the sentence."

"I was drinking my water."

"You were pre-loading the sentence." He pulled the lace tighter anyway, which had to hurt, and reached for his stick. "It's fine. Let's go."

Pascal was already standing at the ridge edge, looking down. In the pre-dawn grey, the valley below was a dark shape, indistinct, like something seen through smoked glass. He had his map but he wasn't looking at it.

"Pascal," I said.

He turned.

"You ready?"

He looked at the valley for another moment. "Yes," he said. He folded the map and put it away. "Stay close when we get to the bottom. And keep quiet."

He said the last part the way you say something you've been planning to say for a while. Not a reminder. A rule.

We went down.

The descent took twenty minutes and was hard going, the slope loose with shale and autumn-slick pine, Rusty managed it in his particular way — carefully, methodically, without complaint, the stick planting and testing before each step like a blind man's cane. Pascal went first to find the safest line and I dropped back to walk behind Rusty without making it look like I was walking behind Rusty.

Halfway down, Bobby appeared on Rusty's other side. Just moved there, without comment, close enough to grab an arm if the ankle went.

Rusty didn't acknowledge this. He just walked between us and let it be.

That's the thing about Bobby Aldridge that I have spent years trying to explain to people who never met him. He didn't offer help. He didn't make a production of caring about you. He just repositioned himself so that if something happened, he would be there. Silently. As a fact. It was the most generous thing I have ever seen anyone do, and he did it constantly, and he never once seemed to know that it was remarkable.

We reached the valley floor.

Something changed at the bottom.

I noticed it before I understood it. A quality of the air, maybe, or the light, or both — something that made the skin on my forearms tighten the way it tightens before a thunderstorm. The trees down here were different from the pines above. Older. Their trunks were massive and dark with damp, the bark deeply furrowed, the canopy so thick overhead that we had gone from the grey morning light to something closer to dusk in thirty meters.

"This way," Pascal said. He moved along what might have been a drainage channel once — a shallow depression in the forest floor, overgrown but still distinct if you knew what you were looking for.

We followed it.

And then the birds stopped.

Not gradually. Not one by one the way they trail off at nightfall. All at once, as if someone had reached up and turned a dial, the forest went silent. The insects with it. Everything. The only sounds were our footsteps, and our breathing and the quiet drag of Rusty's stick through the leaf mulch.

Nobody mentioned it. We all felt it. I watched Bobby's eyes go to the canopy and then back to eye level and stay there.

The temperature dropped. Not much — three degrees, maybe four — but after two days of summer heat, four degrees feels like a hand on your shoulder.

Pascal stopped.

He was looking at something through the trees. We came up beside him and looked.

The bunker at Kilometer Fourteen did not look like what any of us had imagined.

I don't know exactly what I'd been expecting. Something dramatic, maybe — a fortress, a structure that announced its own significance. What we got was the opposite. The bunker was barely visible. It emerged from the hillside so gradually, so organically, that your eye kept trying to read it as geology — a rock formation, a natural rise. Thirty years of ivy and moss had done their patient work. The concrete was the grey-green of lichen, and the lichen was the grey-green of concrete, and the boundary between the man-made and the reclaimed was almost impossible to locate.

Almost.

What gave it away was the angles. Nature doesn't do right angles. Nature doesn't do the specific flatness of a poured surface, the deliberate narrowness of an observation slit. Once you saw those angles, you couldn't unsee them, and then the whole shape of the thing resolved: a long, low structure pressed into the hillside like a fist pushed into dough, maybe forty feet across the face, with reinforced corners and two observation ports and an entrance set into the left end that was half-buried in soil and had a rusted iron door hanging open on one hinge.

The door was open.

We all looked at the open door for a moment.

"Someone's been here," Bobby said.

"Recently?" Rusty said.

Pascal studied the entrance. "The vegetation around the frame," he said. "It's been disturbed. But not today. Maybe not this season." He moved closer, crouching, looking at the threshold. "There are boot prints in the mud inside. Not old. Recent."

"How old?" I asked.

He straightened up. "Recent enough," he said. Which wasn't an answer, but the way he said it made me not want to push for one.

We stood outside the bunker entrance, and nobody moved for a full thirty seconds.

It was Rusty who broke it. He limped forward on his stick, looked at the door hanging on its hinge, looked at the entrance beyond it, and said: "Well. We didn't walk three days on a busted ankle to stand in the woods."

He was right.

We went in.

The entrance was smaller than expected. You had to crouch, all four of us, and then you were inside, and the first thing — the very first thing before your eyes adjusted or your mind caught up — was the smell.

Not rot. Not death. Something older and stranger than either.

It smelled like the inside of a stone wall. Like wet concrete and mineral cold and iron that had been rusting slowly for a generation. And beneath that, something that took me a full minute to identify-tobacco. Old, ghost tobacco, twenty-six years of cigarette smoke absorbed into the concrete and never leaving, released now by our body heat as we moved through. It was the smell of men who had lived here, and it was more unsettling than anything visible, because you can brace yourself for what you can see. You can't brace yourself for a smell.

"God," Rusty said.

"Tobacco," Pascal said. "They smoked constantly in these positions. There was nothing else to do."

"That's — that's still here after all this time?"

"The concrete holds it." He had his flashlight out now, a small military-issue torch his father kept in a kitchen drawer, borrowed without asking. The beam cut a thin channel through the darkness. "It will hold it for another hundred years probably."

We moved deeper.

The corridor was narrow — barely wide enough for two people abreast — with a ceiling so low that Bobby and I could reach up and touch it without fully extending our arms. The walls were rough concrete interrupted by the occasional iron bracket where equipment had been mounted and long since removed. The floor was damp and uneven, and in places where moisture had been seeping for decades the concrete had developed a fine, pale crust, almost crystalline, that crunched softly under our shoes.

That sound — that soft, guilty crunch with every step — made the corridor feel like something that didn't want to be walked through.

We passed an opening on the right: a sleeping alcove barely large enough for a cot, empty now except for a rusted metal frame collapsed against the far wall like something that had given up. I counted the alcoves as we passed. There were four of them. This bunker had housed four men. I thought about that — four men in four alcoves, in this corridor, with those observation slits their only window onto a world that was trying to kill them.

Four men. Four of us.

I didn't say that to the others.

Then Rusty's flashlight hit the ceiling and something exploded.

That's the only word for it. An explosion of sound and movement that filled the corridor from wall to wall, a rushing, leathery, frantic chaos that hit all four of us simultaneously and sent Rusty into the wall and Bobby down on one knee with his arms over his head and me back two steps into Pascal, who grabbed my shoulder and held on.

Bats. A colony of them, maybe forty or fifty, disturbed from their roost by our lights and our warmth, pouring past us in a black wave toward the entrance. The air they displaced was warm and smelled of something animal and ancient. The sound — thousands of tiny leathery wingbeats — was unlike anything I can accurately describe. Like paper tearing, but alive. Continuous. Right at your face.

It lasted maybe eight seconds.

Then they were gone, out through the entrance, dispersed into the morning, and the four of us were standing in the corridor in the ringing silence they left behind, breathing hard.

"*What,*" Rusty said.

"Bats," Pascal said. He was the only one of us who had not flinched. Or if he had, he'd finished flinching before anyone saw it. "Common pipistrelles. They roost in structures like this."

"You could have — that would have been extremely useful information *before—*"

"I didn't know they were there."

"You know every plant that will kill me but you didn't know about the—"

"Rusty," Bobby said. He was standing up, brushing his knee off. His voice was steady, but when the flashlight caught his face I could see he was still pale. "Are you okay?"

Rusty looked at his own hands. He had pressed them flat against the corridor wall when the bats came through, and the wall had left a grey chalk-dust impression on both palms. He looked at the impressions for a moment.

"Yeah," he said. "Yeah, I'm good." He pushed off the wall. His ankle made him wince. "Let's keep going."

The corridor opened into a larger space — the command room, Pascal said — maybe thirty feet square, with a table still in the center that had gone the color of old bone. Iron chairs, their canvas seats rotted away, ringed the table like something formal. A ghost meeting. On the far wall, a clock still hung, its face intact, its hands stopped at six forty-seven. I assumed it was morning.

On the south wall, a series of iron hooks held nothing. On the north wall, two observation slits let in thin blades of outside light that fell across the floor in pale rectangles, and in those rectangles of light I could see the floor more clearly than anywhere else in the room.

Someone had scratched words into the concrete at knee height along the north wall. Not official markings, not stenciled text. Personal. Done with a blade or a nail, the letters uneven and pressed hard, the way you write when you have something you need to leave behind.

I crouched down and put my flashlight on them.

A name: *Werner.* A date: *März 1945.* And beneath that, in smaller letters, something Pascal came and read over my shoulder.

He was quiet for a moment.

"What does it say?" Bobby said.

"*Ich war hier,*" Pascal said. "*Ich liebte sie.*" He paused. "*I was here. I loved her.*"

Nobody said anything.

Bobby put his hand flat on the concrete next to the words and held it there, the same gesture as the dragon's tooth, the same gesture as the pillbox. Making it real. Making sure it counted.

"Werner," Rusty said quietly. The name sat strange in the air of the room, too specific, too present for a place this abandoned.

"Private Werner Hess," Pascal said. None of us had told him the name. He said it the way you say something you've been carrying for a while and are finally ready to put down. "My grandfather knew him. He died here. When the Americans came through." He looked at the scratched words. "He was twenty-two."

I looked at Pascal. He was looking at the wall.

"Your grandfather told you his name," I said.

"He told me everything," Pascal said. "He just told it slowly. Over many years. In pieces." He straightened up. "He felt responsible. He wasn't here when it happened, but he felt responsible." He moved the flashlight beam away from the inscription, toward the eastern wall. "He spent a long time feeling responsible."

The eastern wall.

And that's when we saw it.

It was up higher than I would have looked — chest height, centered on the cleanest section of the wall, where the concrete had taken the least moisture damage. The letters were cut deep and sure, the work of a man who knew he was leaving something that needed to last. The famous bald cartoon face peered over his wall with its long nose and its knowing eyes.

KILROY WAS HERE.

Rusty said nothing. Bobby said nothing. Pascal said nothing.

We all just looked at it.

An American soldier had stood in this exact spot. Had stood here in the smoke and the noise and the specific terror of March 1945 and had taken a knife to the concrete and had left this — this ridiculous, defiant, beloved piece of graffiti that American soldiers left everywhere they went, on every continent, in every theater of the war. *I was here. We were here. You didn't stop us.*

Rusty reached up and put two fingers against the letters.

"He made it," Rusty said. It wasn't a question.

"He made it out," Pascal confirmed. "The Americans took this position on the morning of March sixteenth. The advance moved north by midday."

"He had about ten minutes in here," Bobby said.

"Something like that."

Bobby's eyes dropped from KILROY WAS HERE to the base of the wall. They stopped.

"There," he said.

It was subtle. You'd miss it if you weren't looking, and you'd probably miss it even if you were. Below the cartoon and the words, scratched with the same blade but smaller, tighter, more deliberate — an arrow. Pointing straight down at the floor.

We all looked at it. Then we all looked at the floor below it.

The concrete ended about six inches from the wall. What came after it was earth — compacted, dark, different in color and texture from the rest of the floor. A square of it, maybe eighteen inches across, that was slightly, almost imperceptibly, lower than the ground around it.

Like something had been removed from that space, and the earth had settled over the years into the negative shape of it.

Or like something was still there.

"He buried something," I said.

The sound of my own voice surprised me. It had gone strange in the concrete room — slightly delayed, slightly wrong, like hearing yourself on a tape recorder.

Like your voice was coming from a version of you that was standing two feet behind where you actually stood.

Pascal crouched at the edge of the earthen square. He pressed his palm flat against it, feeling the density, the depth.

"Not deep," he said. He looked up at us. His eyes in the flashlight were very still. "Whatever it is. It's not deep."

We looked at each other, the four of us, in the command room of Bunker 1-14-Gamma with the clock stopped at six forty-seven and Werner Hess's words on the wall and a dead American sergeant's arrow pointing at the ground.

"We dig," Bobby said.

WHAT THE ARROW WAS POINTING AT

"WE NEED SOMETHING TO DIG WITH," I said.

This was not as straightforward as it sounds. Between the four of us we had: Rusty's folding knife, a canteen, Bobby's sketchbook, Pascal's map, the walking stick, and the combined optimism of boys who had not thought through the digging part when they planned the finding part.

"Stick," Bobby said.

Rusty handed it over without argument, which was how I knew he was feeling the ankle. He lowered himself carefully to the floor with his back against the wall and watched while Bobby crouched at the earthen square and began working the stick's end into the soil at the edge.

The earth was compacted but not rock-hard. It moved. Bobby worked methodically, loosening the perimeter first, the way you'd core an apple — around the outside, then in. Pascal and I crouched nearby with our flashlights aimed at the hole. Rusty aimed his from where he sat.

The command room was very quiet.

"I keep thinking about that clock," Rusty said.

"Don't," I said.

"Six forty-seven. That's specific."

"Rusty."

"I'm just saying. Someone was looking at that clock when it stopped and that's the last thing they—"

"*Rusty.*"

He went quiet. Bobby kept digging.

Four inches down, the stick hit

something solid and the sound changed —
a flat, dense knock, metal on metal, that
rang briefly in the concrete room and
then was gone.

We all heard it.

Bobby stopped. He looked at the spot.
Then he set the stick aside and started using his hands, pulling the loosened earth
back, widening the hole. The rest of us
leaned in closer with our lights.

The thing revealed itself slowly, the
way buried things do — an edge first, then
a corner, then the unmistakable shape of a
military ammunition can. Standard issue,
rectangular, olive drab gone brown with
age and moisture. The latching mechanism on top was a C-clamp hasp, the kind
with a rubber seal designed to keep contents dry in a field environment.

It had done its job. Mostly. The outside was corroded and the hasp was rusted
stiff, but the can itself was intact.

"It's a fifty-cal. ammo can," Pascal said.
"German. This is what they used to pack
machine gun belts in for transport."

"Or bury things," Rusty said quietly.

Bobby got both hands around the sides and pulled. The earth held it for a moment — a decade's worth of suction from the settled ground — and then released it with a sound like a boot being pulled from mud, sudden and definitive, he fell back, Rusty caught his shoulder and the can crashed into his lap.

We all looked at it.

The whole situation was suddenly real in a way it hadn't been before. While the arrow was pointing at earth, it was still partly a theory. Now the theory had a handle and corners and thirty years of rust and whatever was inside it, and I was aware that my heart was going considerably faster than normal and that my mouth was dry in a way that had nothing to do with thirst.

"Open it," Rusty said.

Pascal found a piece of rebar in the corner debris — a short length with one flattened end, left from some repair or collapse — and worked the tip into the gap between the hasp and the lid. He applied pressure steadily, evenly, the way you do something that requires patience rather than force.

The hasp groaned. Corroded metal grinding against corroded metal, the sound of something that hadn't moved in a very long time being asked to move. Pascal increased the pressure.

It broke with a sharp crack, the hasp springing away, and Pascal lifted the lid.

The smell came first.

Not rot. Not what you'd expect from something buried for twenty-six years. Something dryer and older — the specific smell of cloth that has been sealed away from air for decades. Museum-smell. Archive-smell. The smell of a thing that has been waiting.

Wrapped in rotted cloth, sitting on a bed of what had once been thin cotton and was now mostly pale fiber, were four coins.

Gold coins.

Even in the combined beams of three flashlights pointed into a metal can, even after everything that preceded this moment, the sight of them stopped all four of us completely. They caught the light and threw it back. Not reflected — *thrown.* The way only gold does. A warm, specific radiance that has nothing to do with the wattage of your light source and everything to do with what gold actually is.

Rusty said something under his breath that I won't repeat here.

Bobby reached out and picked one up. He turned it over slowly. Both sides: a stern profile face on one, an eagle crest on the other, lettering around the rim that none of us could read.

"German," Pascal said. He took the coin from Bobby carefully and angled it in the light. "Gold Mark. Twenty Mark denomination." He checked the date. "1908."

"Nineteen-oh-eight," I said. "That's — that's before the First World War."

"Yes." He turned it over again. "These belonged to someone before the war. Before either war." He set it back with the others. "Someone kept these for a very long time before they ended up here."

I thought about that — a soldier carrying coins that were already old when he was young, coins that had survived one war already and were now surviving a second. Coins that had been someone's savings, or inheritance, or simply the weight of a life carried in a pocket.

Pascal moved the coins aside carefully, and beneath them, wrapped in what had been a piece of canvas but was now more suggestion than material, was a book.

Small. Dark cover. German text, the spine worn to bare board.

"Bible," Pascal said.

He opened it at the front. Something fell out — a photograph, drifting to the floor of the bunker, face-down. I picked it up.

A woman. Standing in front of a house in what looked like summer. Her hand raised to shade her eyes against bright sunlight, her face half in shadow. She was looking at the camera with an expression that was neither smiling nor serious — just present. Just there. Just looking.

No inscription. Nothing on the back. No name, no date.

I have seen that photograph in my mind many times over the years. Every time I try to place her I can't. Some woman who stood in summer sunlight while someone who loved her pointed a camera, and who had no idea that her photograph would end up in a buried can in a German bunker, found by a twelve-year-old boy from a military base who had no business being there.

I handed it to Pascal. He looked at it for a long moment and set it gently on top of the Bible.

Then I saw the Luger.

It was wrapped in the remains of a canvas holster, and when Pascal lifted it clear and unwrapped it, the condition of it was startling. Not pristine — nothing in that can was pristine after twenty-six years of temperature cycling — but close. The mechanism was clean. The grips were dark with decades of handling, worn to the shape of a particular hand. Pascal worked the action carefully and the slide moved with a smoothness that had no right to exist in a buried weapon.

"Someone maintained this," I said.

"Right up until they couldn't," Pascal said.

He set it back in the can without another word.

None of us spoke for probably a full minute.

Rusty broke it, which was right. It was always going to be Rusty.

"Okay," he said. "So. That's real."

"That's real," Bobby confirmed.

"The coins are — those are worth—" He stopped. Recalibrated. "I mean, actual gold. Four of them. Pre-war German gold coins." He looked at Pascal. "Right?"

"Correct."

"So we take them."

A beat.

"We're not *stealing* them," I said.

"From who?" Rusty said. "From the ghost? The ghost of whoever buried them? They've been in a hole in the ground for twenty-six years, Galen. If he wanted them back he had a long time to come get them." He paused. "And the arrow. He *pointed* at them. That's practically—"

"That's not the same as—"

"*Boys,*" Pascal said.

We looked at him.

"We take the coins," he said. "We leave everything else." He looked at the Bible, the photograph, the Luger. "The rest stays. It belongs here." He looked at each of us in turn with an expression that was not a suggestion. "One coin each. And we tell no one. We don't sell them. Not yet. Not for a long time. Agreed?"

Rusty opened his mouth.

"*Agreed,*" Pascal said.

Rusty closed his mouth. Then: "Agreed."

Bobby: "Agreed."

Me: "Agreed."

Pascal put the Bible and the photograph back in the can. He placed the Luger on top. He closed the lid as well as the broken hasp would allow. He set it back in the hole.

"We cover it," he said. "The way it was."

Each of us kept a coin. I put mine in my front jeans pocket and felt the weight of it against my leg, heavier than it had any right to be, and I thought: *this is from 1908. This was someone's.* I thought about all the hands it had passed through to get to mine.

Then Bobby said: "There's something else."

He was pointing his flashlight at the back wall of the command room.

Not the wall with the observation slits. Not the wall with KILROY WAS HERE. The back wall, the one we'd had our backs to the whole time, the one we hadn't looked at carefully because the arrow had been pointing the other way.

There was a door.

Not a proper door — no frame, no hinges. More of an archway, partially blocked with sandbags that had rotted to nothing and left only a residue of dried sand and decomposed burlap. Beyond the archway, a passage led back into the hillside, angling down, going somewhere.

"Secondary tunnel," Pascal said. "Most command bunkers had them. Secondary egress, supply access." He aimed his flashlight into the passage. The beam went about fifteen feet before the darkness swallowed it. "This one goes deeper."

"How deep?" I said.

"I don't know."

We looked at the passage.

We looked at each other.

"We came this far," Rusty said.

"Your ankle," Bobby said.

"My ankle can manage a passage."

"Rusty—"

"*I'm fine,*" he said, with a finality that closed the discussion. He got his stick under him and stood. He was pale with the effort but he was standing. "Lead on, Pascal."

The passage angled down at maybe ten degrees, just enough to feel deliberate, the floor rough-poured and cracked in places where the hillside had settled over the years. The walls closed in slightly as we went, until we were moving in single file with Pascal in front and me behind him and Bobby behind me and Rusty last, his stick clicking a soft rhythm on the concrete.

The air changed as we went deeper. Colder. Stiller. The mineral smell gave way to something else — the ghost of petroleum, old oil, the fossilized memory of machinery.

Pascal stopped. He held up a fist without turning around.

We stopped.

He moved his flashlight to the right wall. Mounted there, still intact after twenty-six years, was an electrical switch panel. Iron housing, German text on the labels, twelve switches in two rows. Every switch was in the off position.

"Power source for the secondary facility," Pascal said quietly. "Run off a generator. Generator's been dead since '45 obviously." He looked at the panel for a moment. "But the wiring might still—" He looked at us. "Stand back."

"Pascal," I said.

"Stand back, Galen."

He reached out and flipped the first switch.

Nothing.

Second switch.

Nothing.

He went down the row. Nothing, nothing, nothing. We breathed again. The panel was dead. I suspected so much after 26 years.

Rusty breathed. And swept his light around the passageway.

"No emergency circuit, nothing." Pascal said. He sounded surprised. He was hoping for a separate battery array. After twenty-six years—maybe?"

We had enough.

Bobby's flashlight swept ahead of us. The passage opened into a cavern.

I've tried to describe this to people over the years and I've never entirely managed it, because the scale of it doesn't fit the context. You're in a hillside bunker. You've been in narrow passages and concrete rooms barely big enough for a cot. Your whole sense of the space has been calibrated to tight and low and close. And then the passage ends and the cavern opens and the scale hits you like a physical force.

It went back perhaps two hundred feet. The ceiling was fifteen feet at the apex of the natural sandstone arch that formed it — the bunker engineers had used an existing cave structure and reinforced and expanded it with concrete and iron. Down both sides, lined up with a precision that suggested someone had a long time and meticulous standards, were vehicles.

Army trucks. Staff cars. Two half-tracks. A motorcycle with a sidecar still attached.

All of it German. All of it military. All of it left exactly as it had been parked. Our light beams bounced off the walls, the ceiling, the equipment.

The tires were flat, gone to cracked rubber after decades, the trucks sitting on their rims. The windshields were covered in a fine grey dust that muted them to opacity. The paint, which would have been grey-green, had dulled to something closer to the color of old bone. Cobwebs connected steering wheels to dashboards, door handles to door frames, one vehicle to the next, a pale lacework that documented twenty-six years of absolute stillness.

Bobby reached out and touched the hood of one of the trucks and pulled his finger back leaving a clean swipe void of thick dust.

Against the far wall: crates. Floor to ceiling. Row upon row. Ammunition crates, fuel cans stacked six high, what looked like field rations, radio equipment still in its packing.

An entire army's capacity to continue, preserved and sealed and never used.

"They were going to come back," Bobby said.

His voice in that cavern was very small.

"Yes," Pascal said. "They thought they were going to come back."

Rusty moved along the nearest truck, his flashlight sweeping the cab. He reached in through the open window and tried the door handle from inside and the door opened with a grinding of rust that echoed through the whole cavern. He looked at us. He looked at the door.

"Don't," Bobby said.

"I wasn't going to—"

"You were."

"I just want to—"

"*Rusty.*"

He closed the truck door. Carefully. Respectfully, almost. He stepped back.

"This is what my grandfather knew about," Pascal said. He was looking at the cavern the way you look at something you've known the shape of for years and are finally seeing in three dimensions. "Not just the bunker. *This.* This is what he said should stay sealed." He paused. "This isn't for us. This is for—" He stopped.

"For who?" I said.

"For the right time. The right people. People who know what to do with it." He looked at me. "We're twelve, Galen."

"Thirteen," Rusty said.

"We're *children*," Pascal said. "And this is a very large thing."

He was right. I knew he was right. The cavern, the trucks, the crates — it was a very large thing, and we were standing in the middle of it with flashlights and two Snickers bars between us, and the smart move was obvious and I knew it.

"We go," I said. "We tell no one about this part."

"Agreed," Bobby said. Immediately.

Rusty looked at the trucks one more time. The row of them, patient and still, waiting for an army that had stopped existing.

"Agreed," he said. "Yeah. Agreed."

We went back up the passage by flashlight,

single file, and I was second-to-last and I was thinking about the cavern, about the crates, about all of it, which is probably why I almost walked into Pascal when he stopped.

He stopped dead. No warning, no signal. Just stopped.

I put my hand on the wall to keep from running into him. Bobby bumped into me from behind.

"Pascal—" I started.

"Quiet," he said.

His voice was different. The specific quiet of someone who has heard something and is still processing what it means.

I listened.

The passage. Our breathing. The distant drip of water.

And then from the command room above us — from the direction of KILROY WAS HERE and the stopped clock and Werner Hess's words scratched in the wall — a sound.

Not a bat.

A footstep.

One footstep, deliberate and weighted, the sound of something with real mass moving on concrete.

We stood absolutely still. All four of us, in the dark passage, not moving. The flashlights off now — Pascal had clicked his off at the first footstep and Rusty and I followed without thinking.

Complete dark. Complete silence.

Then another footstep. Closer.

Then the sound I will hear, I think, for the rest of my life — a sound I knew from base training demonstrations, from the shooting range, from years of living in a world where men carried weapons as tools:

The dry, metallic, unmistakable rack of a rifle bolt being drawn back.

Someone had chambered a round.

They were standing in the command room. Between us and the only way out.

Bobby's hand found my arm in the dark. I didn't move. None of us moved.

We waited.

CHAPTER 6

THE ONE-ARMED MAN

HERE IS SOMETHING THEY DON'T tell you about fear.

The movies get it wrong. In movies, fear is loud. People scream, run, make noise. Real fear — the kind that arrives with the rack of a rifle bolt in a dark concrete passage — is the opposite of loud. Real fear compresses you. It makes you smaller and quieter and extremely still, the way prey animals go still, because somewhere beneath conscious thought the oldest part of your brain has done the math and concluded that stillness is the only available option.

The four of us stood in that passage and did not breathe.

Thirty seconds. A minute. More.

The footstep we'd heard did not repeat. Whoever was in the command room above us was doing the same thing we were doing: listening. Waiting. Trying to build a picture of what was in the dark.

Bobby's hand was still on my arm. I could feel his pulse through his fingertips, going fast. Mine was faster.

Then Pascal moved.

Not toward the command room. Backward. He turned in the passage without making a sound — I don't know how, the passage barely had room to breathe in, but he turned — and his mouth was at my ear.

"Floor," he breathed. One word.

I didn't understand. He put my hand on the passage wall and guided it down, down past knee height to the floor, and I felt it: a seam. A rectangular seam in the concrete, about two feet by three, barely perceptible, the edges worn smooth by decades.

Notausgang. Emergency exit. Standard installation in German command bunkers — a floor hatch leading to a drainage channel that exited the hillside sixty or eighty meters away, designed for exactly this scenario. Every man who built these bunkers planned for the moment when the door was no longer an option.

Pascal had known. Of course he had. His grandfather told him.

He found the recessed handle, a flat iron ring flush with the floor, and pulled. The hatch resisted — twenty-six years of compressed earth on the other side — and then gave, scraping against the frame, a sound that seemed enormous.

Above us, in the command room, the footstep came again.

Closer.

The drainage channel was barely three feet in diameter.

We went through on our stomachs, one at a time, Pascal first, then Bobby, then me, then Rusty who handed his stick through ahead of him and pulled himself forward on his forearms with his bad ankle held up and never made a single sound about it. The channel was concrete, cold, damp, absolutely dark. It smelled of minerals and old water and fifty feet of compressed earth above us.

I am not particularly prone to claustrophobia. I discovered in those three minutes of crawling that I am more prone to it than I had previously understood.

We moved by feel and by the sound of Pascal ahead of us. The channel angled up slightly as it went, and the air changed — less still, the faintest suggestion of outside — and then Pascal's feet disappeared and a grey rectangle of light appeared and I pulled myself through it into the open air and lay flat in the wet grass and breathed.

The emergency exit opened in the drainage ditch below the bunker's east face. We were outside, twenty meters from the bunker's main entrance, hidden by the slope of the land and the thick brush that had grown up around the drainage outlet over three decades. From the bunker entrance we were invisible.

Bobby came through. Then Rusty, pulling himself clear and rolling to his back and staring at the sky for a moment with the expression of a man conducting an internal audit.

"Okay," Rusty said, very quietly. "Okay."

We lay in the ditch and listened.

From inside the bunker: nothing. No pursuit. No shout. The birds had started again somewhere above us, a thrush going through its repertoire, indifferent to our situation.

Pascal was on his hands and knees, looking back at the bunker entrance from the cover of the brush.

"He's still inside," he murmured.

"How do you know?" I breathed.

"Because if he'd followed us he'd already be on us." He watched the entrance. "He knows the passage system. He knows about the floor hatch." He paused. "He let us go."

"He let us — what do you mean he *let us go?*"

Pascal looked at me. His expression was the careful one, the one he wore when he was thinking faster than he was speaking. "He heard us go through that hatch. He heard every sound we made. If he'd wanted to follow, he'd have been through it in thirty seconds." He looked back at the entrance. "He stayed."

"Why?"

Pascal didn't answer. He kept watching the entrance.

Then he did something none of us expected. He stood up.

He stood up from the cover of the drainage ditch and walked out of the brush and stood in the open ground in front of the bunker entrance and said, in German, clearly, at a level designed to be heard inside:

"Mein Großvater hieß Ernst Renard."

My grandfather's name was Ernst Renard.

"Pascal," Bobby said, very quietly. *"Pascal."*

Pascal did not look at us. He kept his eyes on the bunker entrance and waited.

Ten seconds.

Twenty.

The one-armed man stepped out.

He was older than I expected and not at all what I expected, and I have thought many times about why the two things surprised me simultaneously. I think it's because I had been building a picture of him from the boot prints and the foreshadowing and the racked rifle bolt, and the picture I'd built was of something more simply dangerous. What actually emerged from the bunker entrance was more complicated. He was wearing the same heavy work trousers and suspenders as the figure we'd seen across the field three days earlier, squinting toward the tree line.

He was perhaps sixty, perhaps older. Lean in the way of men who have done physical work their entire lives and never stopped. His face was weathered past the point where you could read much from it easily — it required study, and it rewarded study, the way a landscape does. He wore the clothes of a working farmer: heavy trousers, suspenders, boots that had seen decades of use. His left sleeve was folded and pinned at the shoulder. He had managed, over the years, to carry himself in a way that made the missing arm seem less like an absence than simply part of his particular architecture.

The rifle was a German bolt-action,

wartime vintage, and he carried it in his one hand with the relaxed competence of someone who had been carrying rifles since before we were born. It was pointed at the ground.

He looked at Pascal for a long moment.

Then he looked at the rest of us, one at a time. I had the specific uncomfortable feeling of being assessed by someone who was extremely good at assessing things and was not going to tell me the results.

He said something in German.

Pascal answered. The exchange was brief. Then Pascal turned to us.

"He says we should come inside."

"*Inside,*" Rusty said.

"He says we should come inside and we should bring whatever we took from the floor."

A silence.

"He knows," Bobby said.

"He knows," Pascal confirmed.

The man looked at us with an expression of absolute patience. The patience of someone who has been coming to this

hillside for a very long time and has waited through worse than four American
boys deciding whether to trust him.

"He's not going to hurt us," Pascal said.

"How do you know that?" I said.

Pascal looked at the man and then back
at us. "Because he's been here for twenty
minutes and if he wanted to hurt us we'd
already be hurt." He paused. "And because I know who he is."

His name was Dieter Kreuz.

We learned this in the command room,
sitting on the floor with our backs against
the wall beneath the stopped clock, while
Dieter Kreuz stood near the entrance
with the rifle slung on his back — the decision to sling it had been deliberate and
visible, a statement — and spoke to Pascal
in German that Pascal translated in quiet,
even sentences.

He had been coming to this bunker

since 1957. Twelve years after the war. He came four, sometimes five times a year. He checked the main entrance, he walked the perimeter, he went inside and checked the passage and the cavern and the sealed section. He had been doing this for fourteen years.

"Why?" Bobby said.

Pascal translated. Dieter Kreuz answered.

"He made a promise," Pascal said.

"To who?"

Pascal asked. A longer answer this time. Pascal listened, and his face changed while he listened — something moving behind his eyes that he was keeping controlled.

"To my grandfather," Pascal said.

Ernst Renard and Dieter Kreuz had served together on the western frontier in the winter of 1944. Not in this bunker — further north. But they had known each other the way men know each other when they are twenty years old and frightened and spending every day in concrete rooms waiting for an army that is definitely coming.

In January of 1945, as the line contracted and the reassignments came through, Ernst Renard had been moved south. To this sector. To Kilometer Fourteen.

Dieter Kreuz had gone north.

They had not seen each other after that. The war ended. Dieter had come home to his farm — this farm, the one we had skirted the edge of, the one with the sheepdog, the one the tractor sound had come from. six kilometers from the bunker. He had been looking at the ridge above Kilometer Fourteen his entire adult life.

In 1952 he received a letter from Ernst Renard, postmarked Lyon, France. Ernst had survived. He was married, had a son, was working as a schoolteacher. The letter contained three paragraphs of personal news and one paragraph of specific instruction.

"He told Dieter what was in the cavern," Pascal said, translating as the old man spoke. "He said it should not be found until the time was right. He said certain items in the command room had been left by an American soldier during the assault — he didn't know the name—" Pascal paused. "He said those items were not his to keep and were not Dieter's to keep but that they should be protected until the right time." Pascal looked at Dieter Kreuz. "He came to the farm in 1956. My grandfather. He showed Dieter the bunker from the outside. Walked the perimeter. They stood at the entrance." Pascal stopped.

"And?" I said.

"And my grandfather didn't go in," Pascal said. "He never went inside. He said—" He listened to Dieter Kreuz for a moment. "He said there were things inside he had no right to look at."

A silence.

Bobby spoke. "The sealed wall," he said. Not a question.

Pascal looked at him. "Yes."

"Show us," Bobby said.

I want to be precise about what I felt when Bobby said that, because it matters.

Part of me wanted to say *no.* Part of me had been wanting to say no since behind the bowling alley when Rusty first leaned in with his performing-importance voice and started a sentence with *I heard something.* The no was not cowardice. It was the functional part of my brain noting that we were fourteen kilometers from home in a German hillside bunker with a one-armed man and a rifle and gold coins in our pockets and no food and a storm system building to the west and an ankle that needed medical attention.

But there was another part. Smaller, maybe, or maybe larger — I still don't know — that understood what Bobby understood: that we had come this far, and that turning away from the last door was not an option any of us could actually live with.

We'd been twelve once. We would never be twelve again. The sealed wall was right there.

Pascal translated Bobby's request.

Dieter Kreuz looked at Bobby for a long moment. Then he did something unexpected. He reached into his jacket and brought out a small, creased photograph and held it out.

Bobby took it.

It was a class photograph. Thirty or forty children, three rows, the middle-distance formality of a school portrait. The photographer's studio backdrop was visible — a painted garden. The children were dressed carefully, hair combed, sitting very straight.

Dieter Kreuz pointed to a boy in the back row. Second from the right. Dark-haired, serious, approximately twelve years old.

"Werner Hess," Pascal said quietly.

Bobby looked at the photograph. He

looked at it the way he'd looked at the photograph of the woman, and the way he'd looked at the inscription on the wall. Making it real. Making sure it counted.

He handed it back carefully.

Dieter Kreuz returned it to his pocket. Then he turned and walked toward the back passage, the one we'd come through, and picked up a lantern from just inside the entrance — a proper hurricane lantern, a current one, the kind you buy in a hardware store — and lit it with a match from his breast pocket. He looked at us.

We followed him.

The sealed wall was not in the main passage.

It was through the secondary tunnel, past the floor hatch, fifty feet further than we'd gone, where the passage bent sharply left and the ceiling dropped and the walls changed character. Here the concrete was different — rougher, more hastily poured, the aggregate showing unevenly through the surface. No rebar reinforcement visible. A repair job, or a closing job, done quickly by men who were running out of time.

The sealed section was perhaps eight feet wide and floor to ceiling. On our side: the passage. On the other side: whatever was on the other side.

Dieter Kreuz stood before it with his lantern and he put his hand flat against the concrete, and the gesture was so like Bobby's gesture — so exactly like the way Bobby touched the dragon's tooth, the pillbox, the inscription — that I felt something shift in my chest.

He stood there with his palm on the wall for a long time.

Then he spoke.

Pascal translated, sentence by sentence, in a voice I had never heard from him before. Careful and low.

"When the Americans came through on the sixteenth of March, the garrison here was two men. Werner Hess and a sergeant named Bergmann." Pascal paused. "Dieter knew Bergmann from training. He was thirty-five. He was from Munich." Pause. "They held the position for approximately four hours. The Americans took it by direct fire through the observation slits. Neither man came out."

Bobby had the lead toy soldier in his hand. He'd taken it from his pocket without seeming to know he'd done it.

"After the war," Pascal continued, translating steadily, "there was discussion of recovering the remains. There was always discussion. There was never resolution. The records were incomplete. The sector had changed hands multiple times. Eventually—" He stopped to listen. "Eventually the discussion stopped."

"They're still in there," Rusty said.

It was the quietest I had ever heard Rusty say anything.

Pascal asked Dieter Kreuz directly, and the old man looked at Rusty for a moment, and then he nodded. Once.

A silence that had actual weight.

"Werner was twenty-two," Pascal said. He was not translating now. He was just saying it. "He loved someone. He scratched it in the wall because he need-ed to say it and there was no one left to say it to."

Bobby set the toy soldier down at the base of the sealed wall. He placed it care-fully, upright, facing the concrete. Then he straightened up and took the stone out of his pocket — Leo's stone, the smooth river stone that had been in his jacket since February — and he held it for a mo-ment and set it down next to the soldier.

I didn't say anything. None of us did.

The stone and the soldier stood together at the base of the wall in the lan-tern light, and the wall said nothing, and the wall said everything.

We went back to the command room.

Dieter Kreuz sat on the table edge — the table that had been there since 1944, which didn't creak under him, which told me either the table was better built than it looked or he'd sat on it many times before. He set the lantern on the floor. The rifle stayed on his back.

He spoke for a while in German, looking mostly at Pascal, occasionally at the rest of us. Pascal translated.

He knew we had taken something from the floor. He had seen the disturbed earth. He had found the hatch open. He was not, he said, going to take it back from us. He believed, he said — and here his voice carried something that Pascal translated with particular care — that Ernst Renard had always understood that what the American soldier buried would find its way eventually to whoever was meant to have it. That was what the arrow meant.

"Whoever finds it," Pascal translated, "is whoever it was meant for."

He looked at each of us.

He had one condition. The

cavern — the trucks, the equipment, the crates — was not ours to tell. Not yet. The time would come for that, and when it came, the right institutions would be involved and the history would be properly documented. But that time required decisions made by people who were not twelve years old.

"Thirteen," Rusty said, without thinking.

Pascal gave him a look.

"Sorry," Rusty said. "Sorry. Yes. Agreed."

"We tell no one about the cavern," Bobby said. "Not ever, unless he says."

Pascal translated. Dieter Kreuz looked at Bobby for a moment and then nodded, and the specific quality of that nod — the weight of it, the recognition in it — made me understand that he had just decided something about Bobby. I think he recognized the grief. I think people who carry certain things can see it in others.

Then the old man said something final that Pascal did not immediately translate.

"What did he say?" I asked.

Pascal looked at Dieter Kreuz and then at us.

"He said—" He paused. "He said the bunker has been waiting for someone who would leave something as well as take something." He looked at the base of the wall, visible through the passage entrance. The stone. The soldier. "He says the men inside will not be alone now."

Here is what I didn't know, at twelve, standing in that command room:

That Dieter Kreuz would, in fact, contact the appropriate German historical authorities in 1978. That the remains of Werner Hess and Erich Bergmann would be recovered and properly buried with military honors. That the cavern would be documented and its contents transferred to the Bundesarchiv. That a footnote in a 1983 regimental history of the 3rd U.S. Infantry Division would mention the name Raymond Kowalski in connection with Bunker 1-14 Gamma. I would read that footnote in Powell's used bookstore in Portland at the age of sixty-two sitting down on the floor between the shelves not getting up for a while.

What I knew, at twelve, was that we were standing in a concrete room with a clock stopped at 6:47 and a lantern throwing orange light on walls that had heard a lot of history, and that the one-armed man was looking at us with something that might have been gratitude and might have been simple recognition — *yes, this is how it goes, one generation finds what the last one left* — and that I had a gold coin in my pocket that weighed more than gold.

Dieter Kreuz stood. He picked up the lantern. He said one more thing in German.

"Thank you," Pascal translated. "For the stone. And for the soldier."

He walked out through the entrance and into the light and did not look back.

We listened to him go — the even footsteps, the brush of his coat against the entrance frame, the silence that closed in behind him like water.

Bobby was looking at the passage entrance. At the place where the stone and the soldier were.

"He wasn't alone anyway," Bobby said. "Werner. He had Bergmann."

"Yes," Pascal said.

Bobby nodded. He looked at his empty hand — the hand that had held the stone for five months — and closed it. Opened it. Closed it again.

"Okay," he said. "Let's go home."

We collected ourselves. Checked our packs. Pascal's coin was in his breast pocket. Mine was still in my jeans. Bobby had transferred his to his jacket pocket, the same one that used to hold the stone.

Rusty was standing at the entrance,

leaning on his stick, looking at the KIL-ROY WAS HERE inscription one last time.

"Hey, Sergeant Whoever," he said to the wall. "We found it." He pointed his finger at the cartoon face's long nose. "Whatever you were pointing at. We found it."

He turned around. He had the poppy, still, or what remained of it — dried flat now, pressed in his shirt pocket, the petals gone translucent.

He tucked it back in.

"Let's go," he said. "I want that beef stew."

"It's Thursday," I said.

"It's *Friday*," Bobby said.

We all stopped and counted backward.

It was Friday.

It was beef stew day.

Rusty Abernathy smiled the most genuinely happy smile I had seen on him in three days and limped into the light, and the rest of us followed, and the bunker

stood behind us in its hillside and its silence and its long, patient keeping of
things, and the clock on the wall said
6:47, and outside, above the ridge, a red
kite was making slow circles in a sky that
had gone, while we weren't watching, an
astonishing gold.

CHAPTER 7

THE ROAD BACK

THE THING ABOUT CARRYING SOMEthing for a long time is that you stop feeling the weight.

You adjust. Your body compensates, redistributes, builds new muscle around the load. The weight becomes part of your architecture, and you stop knowing it's there because it's been there long enough to feel like you.

Bobby Aldridge had been carrying Leo's stone for five months. Every morning since February he had put it in his jacket pocket. Every night he had put it on whatever surface was beside wherever he was sleeping. It had been in the swimming pool and the commissary and the base theater and three different classrooms and Scout Troop 204 meeting room and the shepherd's hut and the drainage channel under a German hillside. It had been in his hand during the hours he couldn't sleep, which were most of them.

He left it at the base of a sealed wall in a concrete bunker because a German soldier named Werner Hess had scratched *I loved her* in the wall before he died and nobody had been with him since.

We were two hundred meters from the bunker entrance, moving north through the tree cover, when I saw Bobby's right hand go to his jacket pocket.

He stopped walking.

His hand stayed on the pocket. I watched his face go through something — not grief, not regret, something more complicated that I didn't have the vocabulary for at twelve and have spent years since trying to name. Recognition, maybe. The specific recognition of an absence that you chose.

He stood there for three or four seconds.

Then he took his hand off the pocket and started walking again.

Rusty, ahead of us on the trail, didn't look back. But he slowed his pace until Bobby came up alongside him, and then he maintained that pace, and they walked together, and nothing was said about any of it.

That's the thing about those boys. That's the thing I keep coming back to.

We took stock when we hit the first open field north of the ridgeline, spreading ourselves out in the grass and going through packs with the ruthless inventory of people who need to know exactly what they have.

What we had:

Two canteens, both about a third full. Rusty's folding knife. Pascal's map, worn soft at the creases from three days of handling. The four flashlights, batteries going. First aid kit — Bobby's, containing two bandages, a needle and thread, four aspirin, a length of cotton gauze. My notebook, which I had stopped writing in two days ago and which now contained eight pages of the beginning of a story I didn't yet know the end of.

And the coins. One each, in four different pockets.

"Eight kilometers," Pascal said, folding the map. "Roughly. We bear northeast, same general line we came out on but slightly east to avoid the farm." He looked at the sky. It had not improved. The grey thoughtfulness of the western horizon had committed over the past hour to something more decisive — a dark mass that had purpose to it. "We should move quickly."

"Define quickly," Rusty said.

He had his boot off. The ankle had

gone the color of an old plum and the swelling had climbed past the joint and into the lower calf. He was looking at it with the expression of a man who has been telling himself something isn't true and has just run out of road.

Bobby sat down beside him without invitation. He took the cotton gauze from the first aid kit and began to work.

"I don't need—" Rusty started.

"I know you don't need it," Bobby said, in a tone that ended the conversation. He wrapped the ankle in a firm figure-eight, supporting the joint, tucking the end with the precision of someone who had watched his father do field first aid enough times to absorb it without trying. Then he found a branch — straight, about the diameter of a broom handle — and broke it to the right length and used the last of the gauze to pad the top.

He handed it to Rusty.

Rusty looked at it. He looked at Bobby. He took the stick and stood on the ankle and his jaw tightened and then released.

"Better," he said.

Bobby picked up his pack. "Let's go."

We had been walking for forty minutes when the Pfälzerwald *(nature park)* did something strange.

The forest in that region sits over sandstone and limestone — karst geology, riddled with chambers and channels and gaps in the rock that go down to places no one has mapped. Sound behaves oddly in karst terrain. It travels in directions that make no physical sense, bouncing through underground voids, emerging from the earth fifty meters from where it entered. You hear things that have no visible source. You hear things that seem to come from directly below you.

We heard voices.

Not nearby voices. Distant ones,

weirdly clear, emanating from a rock out-crop to our left as though the stone itself was speaking. Two voices, or maybe three, with the clipped cadence of official com-munication.

We stopped.

Pascal had his hand up before I'd even processed the sound.

The voices came again. Clearer now. The static-broken, radio-compressed sound of a military frequency.

"— Sector Gamma, no contact, moving to —"

The rock swallowed the rest of it.

"MP," Bobby said.

Not a question.

We were in the trees but we were not deep in the trees, and the field to our north was open ground, and if a search team was working Sector Gamma — wherever that was — we had approximately no time to think about this.

"Down," Pascal said. "Into the drain-age cut. Now."

We went into the drainage cut, which

was a shallow channel barely deep enough to lie in, and we lay in it. The ground was cold and damp and smelled of recent rain and old leaves and I was face-down in it looking sideways at Rusty whose face was six inches from mine and whose eyes were very wide.

The voices separated from the rock. They had bodies now — two of them, in MP uniforms, working the field edge sixty meters to our north. One had a radio. One had a flashlight that he was running along the tree line even in broad daylight, methodically, each pass five meters further along. They moved with the practised, unhurried efficiency of men who have been doing this for a day and a half and are no longer expecting to find what they're looking for and haven't yet been told to stop.

The radio crackled.

"— All units. Update on the four missing juveniles. Rodriguez, Aldridge, Abernathy, Renard. Last confirmed sighting at—"

Static.

"— parents have been notified search will continue through—"

Static.

The MP with the radio said something back into it. The one with the flashlight finished his sweep and turned around and started back.

We did not move.

I was aware of my own heartbeat in a way I had never been aware of it before — not its speed, exactly, but its location. It was everywhere. My ears, my fingertips, the side of my face pressed into the cold ground of the drainage ditch. Sixty meters away a man with a radio was saying our names in the clipped language of official procedures, and somewhere behind those official procedures were our parents who had not slept, and our mothers who had made our beds three times, and our fathers who were looking at maps and feeling helpless, which was the worst thing in the world for that particular kind of man.

Bobby's name on that radio. Bobby Aldridge. Said the same way you say a file number.

I looked at Bobby. He was flat in the ditch, chin on his hands, watching the MPs through the grass. His face was doing nothing. But his right hand — the hand that had been carrying the stone — was pressed flat against the earth, fingers spread, the way you press against something for balance.

The MPs moved on. Their voices receded. The radio static became part of the forest ambient and then disappeared entirely.

We stayed in the ditch for two full minutes after they were gone.

Then Rusty said, into the ground: "Our parents know."

"Yes," Pascal said.

"They've had the MPs out since—"

"Yesterday, probably," I said. "Maybe yesterday afternoon."

Rusty lifted his head. "My dad is going to—" He stopped. I watched him recalibrate, the way he had to recalibrate sometimes when the thing he was about to say belonged to the old Rusty and not the one who had spent three days in the German countryside and found something real. "My dad is going to be scared," he said. "Not just mad. Scared."

A pause.

"Yeah," I said.

"That's worse," Rusty said.

"Yeah."

Bobby stood up and brushed the ditch mud from his jacket and picked up his pack and his stick.

"Then let's get home faster," he said. And started walking.

The storm came in from the southwest an hour later.

It announced itself the way storms do in that part of Germany in summer — not gradually but all at once, the light going flat and yellow and then gone, the temperature dropping six degrees in five minutes, the first drops enormous and infrequent and testing. Then the clouds opened.

We ran.

Running with Rusty's ankle was not running in any conventional sense. It was a four-person organized chaos — Rusty on Bobby's left side, the stick on his right, Pascal ahead finding the surface, me behind holding Rusty's pack on his back in addition to my own. We made it under the sandstone overhang that Pascal had identified on the map as a shelter option — a ten-foot cantilever of rock that jutted from the hillside above a wide, flat-floored alcove — approximately forty-five seconds before the rain went from heavy to the kind of rain that redefines your understanding of rain.

It hammered the field in front of us. It turned the ground to running water in under a minute. Lightning did its work somewhere to the southwest, the thunder arriving four seconds later, close enough to feel in your back teeth.

We sat against the rock wall of the overhang and watched it and ate nothing because there was nothing to eat and listened to the thunder walk across the hills.

"Beautiful," Bobby said.

Nobody disagreed.

There is a specific quality to being sheltered from something violent. The contrast between the hammering world outside and the stillness inside the overhang made the stillness feel enormous, like something you'd been given rather than something that was simply present. We sat close together without acknowledging that we were sitting close together, four boys and our packs and our secrets and our coins and the rain.

Rusty had the poppy out. It was thoroughly pressed by now, flat and translucent, barely more than a botanical memory of itself. He held it by the stem and turned it slowly.

"She said be careful in the hills," he said.

"She did," Pascal confirmed.

"We weren't especially careful."

"No."

Rusty put the poppy back in his pocket. "Think she does that every day? Goes to that meadow?"

"Probably," Pascal said. "She seemed like a person with a routine."

"I don't even know her last name."

"Moreau," Pascal said. "She told me."

Rusty looked at him. "You didn't mention that."

"You didn't ask."

"Pascal." Rusty stared at him. "You're telling me you had a whole conversation with a girl in a meadow and didn't share the relevant—"

"Rusty."

"*What.*"

"She's French. You don't speak French. What was I going to do, translate your small talk?"

Bobby's mouth moved. Not quite a smile but the precursor to one.

"I speak some French," Rusty said. "I said bonjour. That's French."

"That's one word."

"It's a very good word. It's doing a lot of work."

The thunder moved east. The rain stayed but lost some of its conviction, dropping from catastrophic to merely heavy.

We sat with it.

After a while Bobby said: "I miss him more on good days than bad ones."

No one asked who.

"Bad days, it makes sense," he said. "Good days it doesn't. Something good happens and the first thing I want to do is—" He stopped. "He would have been nine in August." He watched the rain. "He never would've shut up about the gold."

Rusty laughed. Genuine, unguarded, the laugh of someone who didn't mean to and didn't mind.

"Nine-year-old with a gold coin," Rusty said. "Oh, man."

"He'd have told everyone," Bobby said. "Every single person."

"We would've been arrested inside of a week."

"Three days," Bobby said. And he smiled. A real one, the kind that reached his eyes, and in the grey light under the sandstone overhang it was the best thing I saw that entire summer.

He smiled and then he let it go and looked back at the rain.

"I'm glad I came," he said. To no one specifically. To all of us.

"We're glad you came," I said.

He nodded once. That was enough.

The rain stopped as abruptly as it had started, leaving everything dripping and clean and smelling of wet stone and the specific freshness of a world that has been thoroughly rinsed. We emerged from the overhang into the altered landscape and kept moving.

Pascal found the food.

It was on a stone wall at the edge of a farmstead we were skirting — not the farm with the sheepdog, a different one, further north. On the wall: a cloth-covered basket, left in the open.

We stopped and looked at it.

"Don't," I said.

"I'm not going to steal it," Pascal said. He went to the wall and lifted the cloth. Bread. Cheese. Three apples. A small, corked bottle of what turned out to be apple juice, the kind pressed and bottled locally, sharp and cold from the stone.

He covered it again and stood there.

"Take it," Bobby said.

"It's someone's—"

"It's there for travelers," Bobby said. "People leaving food out for travelers is a thing. My grandmother did it. Plate on the wall."

Pascal looked at the basket. He looked at the farmhouse, which was three hundred meters away, no visible movement.

"In Germany," he said slowly, "there is a tradition. Care for wanderers.

Particularly in rural areas. Food left for people passing through."

"There you go," Rusty said.

"It's not exactly the same as—"

"Pascal," Rusty said. "We have walked approximately ten thousand miles on no food. There is food on a wall. The universe is telling us something."

Pascal took the basket.

We ate sitting in the grass behind the stone wall, out of sight of the farmhouse, and the bread was different from the pumpernickel — a lighter wheat loaf, softer — and the cheese was sharp and local and left a clean, specific taste, and the apples were the small, dense, tart kind that German orchards produce. The juice was so cold it made your eyes water.

We ate everything.

"Okay," Rusty said, lying back in the grass with his ankle elevated and his eyes closed. "I've decided. I live in Germany now. I'm not going back."

"Your parents will find that interesting," I said.

"I'll send a note."

"On what?"

He opened one eye. "Fair point." He closed it again. "We'll think of something."

I looked at Pascal, who was watching the farmhouse with a thoughtful expression.

"We're going to have to tell them something," I said. "When we get back. They're going to ask."

"Yes," Pascal said.

"So what do we say?"

He was quiet for a moment. Rusty had opened both eyes now. Bobby was pulling grass stems and braiding them absently, a thing he did when he was thinking.

"We were camping," Bobby said. "In the forest above the base. We found some old concrete structures — bunkers, dragon's teeth. We explored them. Nothing important inside."

"They'll want to know exactly where," I said.

"We got turned around," Bobby said.

"We were lost for a day. We're sorry. We should have told someone. We know." He paused. "That's all true, by the way. We were lost, at points. We are sorry. We should have told someone."

"And the coins," Rusty said.

"The coins don't exist until we're forty," Bobby said. "Agreed?"

"Agreed," I said.

"Pascal?"

Pascal was looking at the middle distance. He'd been looking at the middle distance more than usual since the bunker, and I understood it — his grandfather's photograph, Dieter Kreuz's patient face, Werner Hess's name spoken aloud in a concrete room for the first time in twenty-six years. He had a lot to look at, in the middle distance.

"Pascal," Bobby said again.

"Agreed," Pascal said. He came back from wherever he'd been. "Yes. Agreed."

"Rusty?"

"Oh, completely," Rusty said. "I have

never seen or heard of any gold coins in my entire life."

"Good," Bobby said. He stood up. He shouldered his pack. "Then that's the story."

The last three kilometers were the longest.

This is a thing that happens on any journey — the final approach is always disproportionately hard. Your body knows it's almost over and stops cooperating. Your mind, which has been focused outward for three days, begins to turn back toward the world you're returning to, and the turning is not entirely comfortable. We had been, for three days, people in a story. Now we were about to become people who would be required to explain themselves, and explaining is always smaller than experiencing.

Rusty's ankle had moved past the stage of being manageable by will alone. He was compensating heavily with his left side, and I could see the compensation in his back and shoulder, the way the effort was spreading upward looking for relief it wasn't going to find. He didn't say anything. He walked.

I moved up alongside him.

"Give me the pack," I said.

"No."

"Rusty."

"I said no, Galen."

"It's four pounds. You're walking eight miles on a sprained ankle because you're too—"

"I know what I'm doing."

"You know what you're doing and you're doing it badly."

He stopped. He looked at me with an expression that was several things at once — pride, exhaustion, and something underneath both of those that was neither.

"I need to carry it myself," he said. Quietly. "I just need to do that."

I looked at him.

"Yeah," I said. "Okay."

We walked.

The base perimeter appeared through the trees as the sun was making its final preparations to call it a day, throwing the kind of late-afternoon light that makes everything look briefly like a painting of itself. The chain-link fence. The familiar rooflines above it. The distant sound of — and I am not making this up — an F-4 Phantom on its evening run, right on schedule, the sound arriving before the aircraft and departing after it, same as always.

Except.

We came through the last tree line to the specific section of fence where we had exited four days ago and stopped.

The loose section was gone.

Not repaired — replaced. New wire, bright against the old, stapled to the post with the systematic thoroughness of someone who had found it and understood what it meant and was not going to let it mean that again. The repair was clean and recent, the wire not yet dulled by weather.

"Of course," Rusty said.

We stood there looking at it.

"Another spot?" Bobby said.

Pascal walked the fence line in both directions, looking, testing. He came back.

"Nothing. The whole lower section has been walked and tightened. The search parties." He looked at the main gate, two hundred meters to our right, lit, guarded, the MP on duty visible from here as a silhouette in the fading light.

"The front gate," I said.

"The front gate," Pascal confirmed.

Rusty looked at the gate. He looked at the fence. He laughed — a short, exhausted sound with real humor in it.

"We walked three days in the German countryside," he said. "Found a Nazi bunker, dug up gold coins, met a one-armed farmer, crawled through a drain pipe, and survived a thunderstorm." He gestured at the main gate. "And the scariest thing is walking in the front door."

"Yes," Bobby said.

"That's genuinely the scariest part."

"Yes."

Rusty took a breath. He squared his shoulders over the pack and the stick and the ankle and looked at us each in turn.

"Okay," he said. "We're four kids who went camping and got a little lost. We're sorry. We're home. That's the whole thing."

"That's the whole thing," Bobby agreed.

We looked at each other for a moment. The four of us, at the edge of the fence, with the base on one side and the German countryside on the other and the whole long strange weight of three days pressing equally in both directions.

It wasn't dramatic. Nobody made a speech. There was no ceremony, no formal acknowledgment of what we'd been through and what it meant. We were tired and hungry and Rusty's ankle needed ice and Bobby's jacket was missing its stone and we all had twenty-Mark gold coins in our pockets and mud in our shoes and things we would not say for forty years.

But there was something in the quality of the silence, in the way we were standing, that I recognized even then as significant. The specific quality of four people who have been through something together and know, without discussing it, that the going-through has permanently altered the arrangement.

I have had good friends since. Colleagues, neighbors, people I've known for years. I have no complaints about any of them.

It's not the same. It's just not the same.

Pascal took his map out of his pocket one final time. He looked at it for a moment. Then he folded it and put it in his pack — not his jacket pocket, his pack, where you put things you're done using.

"Ready," he said.

We walked to the main gate.

The MP on duty was a Specialist named Gentry — young, twenty-two maybe, the look of someone three days into a situation he hadn't been trained for and who was going to do his job anyway. He had our names on a clipboard. He looked at us and looked at the clipboard and looked at us.

"Rodriguez," he said. "Aldridge. Abernathy. Renard."

"Yes sir," I said.

He looked at us for a long moment. The mud, the packs, the walking stick, the general condition of four boys who had been outdoors for three days.

He picked up his radio.

He said: "Sergeant Wilkes, this is

Gentry at Main Gate. I've got your four missing juveniles." A pause. "Yes, sir. All four. They're walking." Another pause. "No, sir. Walking. On their own feet." He listened for a moment and his expression did a complicated thing. "I'll tell them, sir."

He put the radio down and looked at us.

"You're in a significant amount of trouble," he said.

"Yes sir," I said.

"Your parents have been notified. They're on their way." He looked at Rusty's ankle. "Medical is also on their way."

"Thank you," Bobby said.

Specialist Gentry looked at Bobby for a moment with the expression of a young man encountering something he didn't have the category for. There was something about Bobby — the steadiness of him, the absolute absence of performance — that tended to produce that reaction in people.

"Welcome back," Gentry said.

He stepped aside.

We walked through.

The base closed around us like something familiar. The smell of it — JP-4 and cut grass and commissary and the low, constant hum of generators — was the smell of every morning of our lives, and after three days of pine and rain and mineral cold it hit like memory, which I suppose is what it was.

I want to tell you that coming home felt uncomplicated. That the relief was clean and the trouble was worth it and we walked back onto that base like heroes returning with a prize.

That's not how it felt.

It felt like the end of something.

Rusty was limping badly now that he'd stopped managing his gait for appearance. Bobby was walking with his hand occasionally going to his jacket pocket and finding nothing and dropping again. Pascal had the faraway look he'd been wearing since the bunker, the look of someone filing things into categories that had been permanently rearranged. I was watching all of them, the way I always watched them, storing it up.

The lights of the housing block came on ahead of us, one after another, and the sound of a jeep came from the east, and somewhere in the direction of our particular row of houses a door opened.

I won't describe the reunions. You can imagine the reunions. They were what you'd expect and more than you'd expect and several of them made sounds I had never heard from adult people before, sounds that had been compressed for two and a half days into the specific frequency of parental terror and were now being released.

My mother's hands on my face. Her voice saying my name not as a word but as a physical act, something she needed to do with her body.

I have tried to think about what it cost her, that night. I am sixty-five years old and I still don't have the full measure of it.

Later — much later, after the medical examination and the ice pack on Rusty's ankle and the firm, deliberately controlled voices of various fathers and one long conversation with the base commander that none of us will ever entirely be able to account for — I sat on the edge of my bed in my room.

The room was the same. Obviously, it was the same. It had been three days. My model of a Spitfire on the desk, my bookshelf, the Hank Aaron poster on the wall. The same room I'd grown up in, or whatever version of growing up you can do in two-year rotations.

I put my hand in my pocket and took out the coin.

It sat in my palm in the lamplight, and it did the thing gold does — threw the light back, warm and specific, from a depth the metal had no business having.

> Sixty-three years ago. Someone had carried it through two wars. An American sergeant had buried it in 1945 with an arrow pointing down. And here it was.

I closed my hand around it.

Outside my window, somewhere on the block, I could hear Rusty's father's voice — not the words, just the tone, the controlled anger that I recognized from years of living around military men, the particular register that meant: *I'm saying this calmly because I've decided to say it calmly and not because any part of me is calm.* And under it, quieter, Rusty's voice giving the story. The camping story. Getting turned around. Being sorry.

I heard it hold up.

I thought about Bobby, in his room, his hand going to a pocket that was lighter than it had been. I thought about Pascal, who had come home to something larger than he left with — not the coin, not the cavern, but the completed shape of a story his grandfather had been telling him in pieces for years, the story now whole and real and his.

I thought about Dieter Kreuz, walking home across four kilometers of German countryside to his farm, to his dog, to whatever a man like that did at the end of a day like this. Sitting down, maybe. Looking at the ridge.

I thought about Werner Hess.

Ich war hier. Ich liebte sie.

I was here. I loved her.

I put the coin on the desk next to the Spitfire. I lay back on my bed with my shoes still on.

From somewhere across the base the F-4s were doing their night run, right on

schedule, the thunder of them rolling
through the dark and fading north.
　　Same as always.
　　Nothing at all the same.

CHAPTER 8

WHAT WE KEPT

My father came into my room at eleven o'clock.

He knocked first, which was not something he always did, and I understood from the knock that this was going to be a specific kind of conversation — not the loud kind, not the *you are in serious trouble* kind, but the kind that required the courtesy of a knock because he had decided to approach it as a man talking to another person rather than a father talking to a child who had done something wrong.

He sat on the desk chair. I sat up

on the bed. The coin was on the desk six inches from his elbow and I did not look at it.

He was quiet for a moment. He had the face of a man who had spent two and a half days doing the calculations — the terrain, the weather, the German countryside, four boys, no supplies — and who had arrived at enough possible outcomes that the real one, the one where I was sitting on my bed with mud on my shoes, required some adjustment.

"I'm not going to yell," he said.

"Okay," I said.

"I want to. I want to very much." He looked at his hands. "But I'm not going to, because I don't think it would accomplish anything, and because—" He stopped. In the silence I could tell he was angry. It was not a long time, but it felt like an eternity. He just sat there looking at me, his hand folded in his lap, straining. He started again. "Because when I was about your age I did something similar, and my father yelled, and all I remember from that conversation is the yelling and none of the content."

I hadn't known that. I filed it away.

"So," he said. "Tell me."

I told him the camping story. The same story Bobby constructed at the stone wall — we went into the forest, found bunkers, got turned around, were lost for a day, came home. I told it the way I had rehearsed it, which was carefully, because the best lies are the ones that are mostly true. We had gone into the forest. We had found bunkers. We had been genuinely lost at points. We were genuinely sorry.

He listened to the whole thing. When I was done he was quiet for a moment, and in that quiet I saw him deciding something. Not whether to believe me — I don't think he entirely did — but whether to push further. Whether the specific details were what mattered or whether the fact of my sitting there, alive and home and able to tell the story, was the thing that mattered more.

He was a good man, my father. He made the right call.

"Your mother," he said. "When you see her tonight, before you sleep. You go to her and you say goodnight. You look her in the eye when you do it."

"Yes sir."

"Not for me. For her." He stood up. He looked at me for a moment. "You scared us, Galen."

"I know."

"Do you?"

I thought about the MP's radio. *Rodriguez, Aldridge, Abernathy, Renard.* Our names in official frequency. My mother making my bed three times.

"Yes," I said. "I really do."

He nodded once. He walked to the door.

"Dad."

He stopped.

"When you were my age," I said. "What did you do? The thing like what I did."

He looked at the door frame for a moment. Then he said: "I went somewhere

I wasn't supposed to go. With people I trusted." He paused. "And it was worth it."

He closed the door behind him.

I sat in the silence he left. The coin was on the desk, throwing its quiet light. I looked at my father's closed door for a long time and I thought: *I am going to remember this moment.* I thought it consciously, deliberately, the way you almost never think about memory while you're inside it. I thought: *put this away carefully. You're going to need it later.*

I went and found my mother in the kitchen and looked her in the eye and said goodnight.

She held my face in both hands and didn't say anything. She didn't need to.

The pact held.

This is the thing I am most proud of, looking back. Not the navigation or the bunker or the coins or any of the external things. The pact. Four twelve and thirteen-year-old boys, under the sustained pressure of frightened parents and a base commander and an MP investigation that lasted three days, telling the same story in four different rooms to four different sets of adults and never once contradicting each other.

We had not coordinated beyond what Bobby said at the stone wall. We had not rehearsed specifics or divided responsibilities or established a hierarchy of who knew what. We had simply agreed, in the grass behind a farmer's wall with the remains of someone's bread and cheese in our hands, that this was the story.

And we kept it.

The base commander — Colonel Cook, a man whose default expression suggested he was constantly solving an equation — called each of us in separately over the following two days. He was not unkind, but he was thorough, and he had the specific skill of very long silences that he used in place of follow-up questions, silences that were designed to make you fill the space with something you hadn't meant to say.

I sat through three session with the Colonel without filling the space.

Rusty, on crutches, sat through one so long that he reportedly said, "Sir, I can do this all afternoon, my ankle's not going anywhere," which was either the bravest or the most reckless thing said in that office that week, and which Colonel Cook apparently received with something that was almost a smile.

Pascal answered every question precisely and completely and in a way that was technically accurate in every particular and revealed nothing that mattered.

Bobby simply told the truth, minus the parts that weren't the base commander's business. When Colonel Cook asked what they had found in the bunkers, Bobby said: "Mostly old equipment and some inscriptions on the walls." Which was entirely accurate. When the Colonel asked why they had gone, Bobby said: "We were curious about history." When the Colonel asked if they would do it again, Bobby looked at him steadily and said: "No, sir. Not without telling someone first."

The *not without telling someone first* was the detail that closed it. It sounded like accountability. It was accountability. It was also a very careful formulation that did not include the word *never*.

We were grounded for two weeks. Rusty was grounded for three, on the logic that his was the original idea. He accepted this as fair.

The coins stayed hidden.

Two weeks after we got back, on the last Saturday before school started, the four of us were in the Scout meeting room.

It was Bobby who had called us there, with the specific economy he used for important things — a note passed at lunch to each of us that said only *Saturday, two o'clock, Scout meeting room,* and signed with his initials. We all came and sat on the floor the way we had sat looking at the German maps three weeks earlier.

Bobby had something in his hand. He set it in the middle of the floor.

It was a round river stone. Not Leo's stone — that stone was at the base of a sealed wall in Bunker 1-14-Gamma, which is where it was going to stay. This was a different stone, similar size, similar smoothness, picked from the stream bank behind the housing block. He'd found it that morning.

"I'm not going to keep a stone," he said. "I don't need to keep a stone." He looked at it. "But I needed to put something in the middle. So here's a stone."

None of us asked him to explain further.

"I want to say something," Bobby said. He looked at each of us in turn. "I want to say it out loud, in front of you, and then we don't have to talk about it again." He paused. "What we did — what happened out there — that's ours. Everything. The bunker, the coins, the man, the wall, all of it. I don't care if I'm eighty years old. I don't care what happens. It's ours." He let it settle. "And you're mine. All three of you. Whatever happens after this, wherever we end up. That doesn't change."

He said it simply, the way Bobby said everything that mattered. No drama, no ceremony. Just the words, and the stone in the middle of the floor, and the four of us around it.

Rusty cleared his throat. He looked at the ceiling. He looked back down.

"Yeah," he said. "Same."

Pascal nodded once. Then he reached into his breast pocket and brought out his coin and placed it next to the stone. Bobby placed his beside Pascal's. I placed mine. Rusty set his down last, completing the circle.

Four coins around a river stone on the floor of the Scout meeting room in Zweibrücken, Germany. September, 1971.

We left them there for one full minute — long enough to count as a ceremony, short enough to keep from feeling foolish — and then we each picked our coin back up and put it away.

"Also," Rusty said, standing on his boot and his recovered ankle. "For the record. I would do it again."

"I know," I said.

"I'm just saying."

"We know, Rusty," Bobby said.

"Good." He picked up his crutch — he was almost off it now, the ankle healing in the grudging way of ankles — and looked around the Scout meeting room. At the footlocker where the maps had been. At the bare floor where we'd spread them three weeks ago and put our fingers on Kilometer Fourteen and said: *there.*

"Good summer," he said.

"Yeah," Bobby said. "Good summer."

We went out into the September afternoon, and the F-4s were doing their thing, and the commissary smelled the way it always smelled, and somewhere across the base a drill sergeant was yelling about something that had nothing to do with us, and it was the same base it had always been, and we were not the same people.

That's the only way I know how to say it.

Same world. Different people.

We walked out together into it.

EPILOGUE

I HAVE TOLD THIS STORY TO FOUR
people in my life prior to writing it down.

The first was my wife, Carole, on our
third date in 1998. I told her the short
version — four boys, a German bunker, something we found, a pact. She
listened without interrupting, which is
one of the reasons I married her. When
I was done, she said: "Do you still have
it?" I said yes. She said: "Good. Don't
sell it." I didn't.

The second was my two sons, at
twelve years and ten-year-old, which
felt like the right age. They listened
with the quality of attention children only give to things that feel

genuinely dangerous. When I finished my older asked: "What happened to the other guys?" I said I'd tell them when they were older. I'm telling they are older now, I suppose, along with everyone else.

The fourth was Bobby — Major Bobby Gene Aldridge Jr. USMC Ret., 50, a resident of Arnold, died on April 18, 2010, at home, surrounded by his loving family. Born on October 22, 1959 in Germany, Bobby lived an adventurous and well-traveled military life, both as a child, a Brat thru and thru, and as an adult. He joined the United States Marine Corps in 1979 and retired in 1999 after twenty years of service. During his time in the Marine Corps, Bobby graduated from the University of Colorado in 1984 with a BS in Electrical Engineering and received his master's in electrical engineering in 1992 from Naval Post Graduate School in Monterey, CA. His love for the service never faded and he became Deputy Director of Research & Development at the U.S. Naval Academy in 2001. Bobby was a true family man and spent most of his time with his wife and three children. He enjoyed family vacations to Breckenridge, Colorado, beach vacations to Wrightsville Beach, NC and sporting events of all kinds. He was baptized in December of 2005 and walked closely with God until his passing. He is survived by his wife of 32 years, Laurene E. Aldridge of Arnold; his son and daughter-in-law, Bobby and Courtney Aldridge of Pasadena; his daughter and son-in-law, Courtney and Bryan Parfitt of Arnold; his daughter Jacquelyn Aldridge of Arnold; two grandchildren, Camryn E. Aldridge and Lucas W. Aldridge; mother, Alice Aldridge of Oklahoma City, OK; two sisters, Susan Rawls of Oklahoma City, OK and Patricia Bart of Dallas, TX; brother, Kenneth Aldridge of Dallas, TX; parents-in-law, Gordon and Kathryn Miller of Frisco, CO. He was my best friend.

I think about Bobby at twelve, placing that stone with the same steadiness he brought to everything — the same hands, the same absolute absence of performance. I thought: *this is who he was, before and after and always.* The boy who repositioned himself next to you in case you needed catching. The boy who told the truth and withheld what wasn't yours to hear. The boy who carried things until he found the right place to set them down.

Laurene sent me his coin last year. It came in a padded envelope with a note that said: *He told me about this. He said you'd know what it means.* I put it on my desk next to mine. Two German gold coins from 1908, side by side, in an office in Portland, Oregon. I look at them every day.

Rusty lives in south Florida.

He is a land developer, which will surprise no one who knew him at thirteen — he was always a person who saw what a space could become rather than what it was. He has been married to the same woman, Donna, for thirty years. They have three kids and four grand-children and a house with a pool and a workshop where Rusty builds furni-ture on weekends, and wrestles alligators which is also not surprising. He always needed his hands busy.

His father's belt buckle is on his work-shop wall. Framed, actually, in a shadow box above the workbench. His kids know the story of the commendation in Korea, because Rusty told them, because that's what you do with the things you decide belong to you.

We connect me every few months on Facebook, always at night, always start-ing with: "Hey. Remember when —" and then whatever it is he's been thinking about. We have talked about the bunker many times over the years, in pieces, in the way you talk about something that's too large to address all at once. Last fall he said: "You know what I think about sometimes? The cave with all that equipment." He paused. "I think about that a lot."

"Me too," I said.

"What do you think it means?"

"I think it means some things hold longer than they have any right to," I said.

He was quiet for a moment. "Yeah," he said. "Yeah, that's it."

He still has his coin. I asked him once if he'd ever thought about selling it. He sounded genuinely offended.

Pascal Renard teaches European history at the University of Lyon.

He specializes, perhaps predictably, in twentieth century Western European conflict and its material legacy. He has published four books. The second one, a study of the Westwall fortifications and their post-war cultural significance, contains in its acknowledgments a single cryptic sentence: *To three Americans who found their way to Kilometer Fourteen in the summer of 1971, and knew what to leave behind.* His academic colleagues have apparently asked about it and he has apparently told them nothing.

We see each other every two or three years — he comes to Portland occasionally for conferences, and I've been to Lyon twice. He is, at sixty-six, recognizably the boy from behind the bowling alley: the same quality of stillness, the same precise economy of language, the same habit of being right without making a production of it.

His grandfather's photograph is on his desk. The German woman squinting into summer sunlight, her hand raised to shade her eyes, one half of her face in shadow. He doesn't know who she was. He has done some research and come close, he thinks, but he hasn't pushed it to a conclusion. I asked him once why not. He said: "Some things are better as questions."

He told me two years ago that in 1978, Dieter Kreuz contacted the German Federal Archive. That the remains of Werner Hess and Erich Bergmann were recovered and interred with military honors in the German War Graves Commission cemetery at Bitburg. That the cavern and its contents were subsequently documented and transferred to the Bundesarchiv. That the process took four years and was handled with complete discretion, the way Dieter Kreuz handled everything.

I asked Pascal how he felt when he heard.

He was quiet for a moment. Then he said: "I felt like my grandfather had finally finished his sentence."

Werner Hess's grave, Pascal tells me, has flowers on it regularly. He doesn't know who leaves them. He has a suspicion, but he hasn't confirmed it, and I don't think he intends to.

Some things are better as questions.

In the fall of 2022, I went back to Zweibrücken.

The base is long closed — the U.S. Air Force left in 1991, and the land has been converted to civilian use, a business park and a small regional airport and a housing development where the old barracks used to be. The bowling alley is gone. The commissary is gone. The baseball diamond is a car park.

But the fence line is still traceable if you know where to look, and the hills to the south are unchanged because hills take longer to change than people, and I drove out on a Tuesday morning October 22. and parked at the end of a farm track and walked.

I'm sixty-three. The walk took longer than it did at twelve. My knees had opinions. I took the same general line we'd taken that July morning forty-eight years ago, through the fields and past the dragon's teeth — still there, many of them, the concrete slowly losing its argument with the earth — and into the old-growth pines where the birds stop and the temperature drops.

I found the drainage channel.

I found the emergency exit, half-buried now, the iron ring long gone to rust.

I stood outside the bunker entrance for a while without going in. The entrance is officially marked now — a small historical commission plaque in German and English, noting the structure's date of construction and its role in the Westwall defensive network. The door has been properly rehung. There's a padlock, which I had anticipated. Pascal had made a call on my behalf, and the key was waiting with the local historical society in Einod.

I went in.

The tobacco smell was still there. Fainter, barely a memory of itself, but there. The clock was still on the wall, hands still at 6:47. The hooks on the south wall still held nothing.

Werner Hess's inscription was still there.

Ich war hier. Ich liebte sie.

I stood in front of it for a long time. I thought about Werner at twelve in the school photograph, hair combed, sitting very straight. I thought about Werner at twenty-two in this room, in March, with the tanks coming.

I thought about Bobby putting his hand flat against the concrete. Making it real. Making sure it counted.

I looked at the eastern wall.

KILROY WAS HERE was still there. Deep and sure and permanent, the cartoon face peering over its wall with its long nose and its knowing expression that says: *I was here before you. I'll be here after.*

Below it, the arrow.

I crouched down and looked at the floor. The earthen square was gone —

the historical survey had found the depression, catalogued it, documented the disturbance. They noted in their report that the original contents of whatever had been buried there had apparently been removed some time before the survey. They listed it as an open question.

I put my hand flat on the floor where the can had been.

Cold concrete. Stone. The specific stillness of a place that has been waiting a very long time and has learned patience the way only places can learn it: completely, without effort, without expectation.

I stayed like that for a while.

Then I reached into my jacket pocket and took out Bobby's coin — the one Laurene sent me — and I held it for a moment, and I set it down at the base of the eastern wall, next to the arrow.

I left it there.

I went back up the passage in the dark, by feel, and out through the entrance, and into the October afternoon.

The trees were turning. The sky was that specific German blue. Somewhere above the ridge a red kite was making slow circles, the same as always.

I walked back to the car. I drove to the airport. I flew home to Portland, to Carole, to my desk with its one remaining coin and the two pages I'd written and been unable to finish for forty years.

I finished them.

I never had friends like those boys. Those "Brats." Not before and not since and not ever. I know that now the way you know things that took too long to learn — completely, without argument, with a specific grief for the years you spent not knowing it clearly enough.

Bobby is buried in a cemetery outside Arnold VA. with one of his daughter drawings laminated and left against the stone by a woman who knew, even at four years old, that he was someone worth drawing for.

The sealed wall at Kilometer Fourteen is no longer sealed. Werner Hess and Erich Bergmann are properly buried. Dieter Kreuz is gone — he died in 1997, his farm passing to a nephew. His dog is gone, the sheepdog that found us in the field and barked and changed our route. The basin with Elodie's wildflowers is still there, if you know where to look, and every summer the poppies come back.

The gold coin on my desk is worn smooth on one face from fifty years of being held. I hold it when I'm working, the way some people hold worry beads, the way Bobby held a smooth river stone. I don't know if that means something. I think it probably means something.

There are things you carry your whole life that you don't know you're carrying until the day you set them down and feel the difference. There are things you leave behind that stay with you longer than anything you kept.

We were four boys in the summer of 1971, behind a bowling alley on an American army base in Germany, and Rusty Abernathy leaned in — he always leaned in — and said *I heard something,* and the whole rest of it followed from there.

I wouldn't change a single step.

Not one.

The End.

HECTOR M. RODRIGUEZ GREW UP as a military brat, living and moving across the world before putting down roots in the Pacific Northwest. He is the author of ten books spanning memoir, literary fiction, children's literature, and experimental prose, including *The Awkward Optimist: A Guide to Human Connection*, *The Path Taken* — a memoir of the Camino de Santiago — and *The Most Excellent Adventures of Bang and Clang*, a children's series about two raccoon brothers navigating the moral questions of growing up.

He is a disabled veteran of the U.S.

Army and spent a long career with the U.S. Department of Energy before turning full-time to writing and community. He teaches life story writing at Linn-Benton Community College, hosts *The Write Time: Inkwell Interviews* — a podcast dedicated to conversations with authors about the craft and purpose of storytelling — and leads children's literacy initiatives through the Kiwanis of Corvallis, Oregon, where he served as president and was named 2025 Kiwanian of the Year. He is a dedicated SMART reader devoting time helping children develop and improve reading skills.

He is a former Scoutmaster and merit badge counselor with Scouting America, and in 2024 fulfilled a fifty-three-year promise to himself by completing a twelve-day trek at Philmont Scout Ranch in New Mexico.

The Summer of '71 is his most personal novel — a tribute to every child who grew up between countries, every soldier who kept a long vigil in a cold place, and every friend who was lost too soon.

He lives in Oregon with his wife and moody Siamese cat named Kai.

www.ingramcontent.com/pod-product-compliance
Lightning Source LLC
Chambersburg PA
CBHW051521150726

47997CB00001B/335